What happens on the scavenger hunt . . .

"She's free, I'm free, and after spending an entire weekend with me, how will she be able to resist?"

"Do you want a list?" Ryan asked.

"Ha ha." Seth made a face at Ryan. "Look, just help me figure out how to get us all on the same team, okay, and we'll figure the rest out as we go along."

"We could call the girls and tell them we want to partner up with them," Ryan suggested, but Seth shook his head.

"That's too obvious. We need to be subtle if this is going to work." Seth leaned closer to Ryan, and spoke in what he hoped was a very profound, insightful voice. "Think like the fox, and you'll get the chicks."

Ryan looked at Seth, his expression deadpan once more. "Yeah, now I'm not so sure *I* want to be on the same team with you."

**Get inside *The O.C.* with the stories
you won't see on TV**

Bait & Switch

Mexico City   New Delhi   Hong Kong   Buenos Aires

Bait & Switch

by Aury Wallington

Based on the television series created
by Josh Schwartz

SCHOLASTIC INC.

New York   Toronto   London   Auckland   Sydney
Mexico City   New Delhi   Hong Kong   Buenos Aires

No part of this work may be reproduced in whole or in part, stored in a retrieval system, or transmitted in any form or by any means, electronic, mechanical, photocopying, recording, or otherwise, without written permission of the publisher. For more information regarding permission, write to Scholastic Inc., Attention: Permissions Department, 557 Broadway, New York, NY 10012.

ISBN 0-439-74570-5

Published by Scholastic Inc.

SCHOLASTIC and associated logos are trademarks and/or registered trademarks of Scholastic Inc.

12 11 10 9 8 7 6 5 4 3 2 1   5 6 7 8 9/0

Designed by Louise Bova
Printed in the U.S.A.
First printing, September 2005

Bait &
Switch

1

"Pool parties suck," Summer said, wincing as the manicurist snipped at her cuticles with small, sharp scissors. "Your hair gets messed up, the food sits out in the sun all day, and there's always some stupid boy who thinks it's funny to splash everyone who walks by."

"She's right," Marissa agreed. She leaned forward in her chair, awkwardly keeping her fingers submerged in the little bowl of soaking solution, and looked at the other girls. "Besides, we have pool parties all the time. We need to think up something different."

The five girls who made up Harbor's social committee had arranged to meet at the Newport Day Spa to get manicures and brainstorm their next big summer event. So far, their nails were looking great, but their ideas needed some work.

"We could have a dinner dance," suggested Liesl, a tiny blond girl whose flippy hair and pug nose made her look more like a Disney character than an actual person.

"Yeah, *that's* different," Summer said, rolling her eyes. "You guys, the whole school counts on us to keep the summer from being a long, hot, boring drag. But we haven't had a party since the Farewell Formal in June. Another dinner dance, by the way," she said, casting a sideways glance at Liesl. "We need to think up something exciting."

"What about a barbecue?" Jenna asked, frowning in embarrassment as the manicurist attempted to file her badly bitten fingernails.

"That's as bad as a pool party," Summer said. "There are bugs everywhere, you reek of sunscreen —"

"Okay, then what about Monte Carlo Night?"

Marissa considered this. "I don't know. The last time we had a Monte Carlo Night it didn't go so well."

She looked down, trying to push the image of Ryan's mom, drunk and sprawled on the floor by the blackjack tables, to the back of her mind. She didn't know if Ryan had seen or talked to his mom in the two years since then, but she was pretty sure he didn't want to be reminded of the spectacle she'd made of herself.

Summer, who was reliving that moment, too, knew that Marissa wouldn't want to risk hurting Ryan, so she chimed in. "Besides, Monte Carlo Night makes us seem kind of ancient, don't you think? Like, my stepmonster would be into going. Let's think up something else."

"But I like the idea of doing something for

charity again," Marissa said, "Just something different than Monte Carlo night."

Tracy, who was getting her nails painted the same shocking pink as the retro-punk stripe in her hair, took a noisy slurp of her diet Coke. "We could build a house for Houses for Friends," she suggested.

"We're supposed to be trying to avoid being hot and bored," Summer reminded her.

But Marissa had straightened up in her chair, her eyes sparkling, a big smile spreading across her face. "That's it!" she said. In her excitement, she waved her hands, flicking a shower of nail softener over the other girls.

"Coop. You can't be serious," Summer said. "Have you ever even picked up a hammer?"

"I didn't mean we should build a house," Marissa answered. "But I said we should do something for charity, and I know just the thing."

"Donkey basketball would be totally fun," Liesl told the group, her eyes getting even wider and more Bambi-like. "My brother's school had a tournament, students against the faculty, and it was hilarious."

"Not donkey basketball!" Marissa said firmly. "A scavenger hunt."

The girls looked at one another. A scavenger hunt actually sounded promising. Seeing she had their attention, Marissa elaborated.

"All these different charities send my mom press releases for her magazine, and one of them was from the Dream-to-Share foundation. They're having a three-day-long scavenger hunt in Los Angeles next weekend. A bunch of different high schools are doing it, and the money from the entry fees goes to help kids with cancer or whatever."

"That could be cool," Summer said. She stuck her freshly glittered nails under the dryer. "And since we'll be in L.A., if it sucks we can blow it off and go shopping."

"It won't suck," Marissa said. "It'll be great. It'll be . . . an adventure."

"I'm in," Tracy said.

"Me too," Jenna said, absentmindedly gnawing on a corner of her newly painted pinky. "I love scavenger hunts."

Marissa gave Liesl a steely glance. "Agreed?"

"Oh." Liesl looked crestfallen for a moment, then shrugged. "Agreed!"

"Perfect," Marissa said, admiring her manicure. "This is going to be the best weekend ever."

"Seth!" Ryan ducked and grimaced as a shard of toenail flew past him. "Do you have to do that here?"

Seth looked up from his seat on the edge of Ryan's bed, a pair of nail clippers poised over his big toe. "Where else should I do it?"

"Your own room? The bathroom? Anywhere other than the pool house?"

"But I need to talk to you. So unless you want to come into the bathroom with me —"

4

"No," Ryan said.

"Then I guess I'll have to do this here." Seth clipped another toe, then looked up at Ryan. "You know, Ryan, there's nothing wrong with good grooming. Pride in your appearance can get you far."

"Seth!" Another nail shard whizzed past Ryan's face, landing on top of his trig book. Disgusted, Ryan flicked it into the trash can. "That's it! Either stop that or get out."

"Fine." Seth folded up the clippers, taking a surreptitious peek at Ryan's toes, poking out of his Puma sandals. "You could borrow these, you know, if you wanted to take care of that cuticle situation."

Ryan gave him a look, and Seth quickly slipped the clippers in his pocket. "Okay, they're your feet," he said in a supercasual voice. "But I personally will just feel better knowing that my toenails aren't going to be scratching Summer while we're having sex this weekend."

Seth clocked Ryan out of the corner of his eye to gauge his reaction. Ryan did not look impressed. Seth tried again.

"I said —"

"Oh, I heard what you said," Ryan informed him. "But it's never going to happen. You aren't going to have sex this weekend."

"Yes, I am," Seth insisted. "I have a plan."

"No, you aren't," Ryan answered. "And if by some miracle you do, it certainly won't be with Summer."

"But my plan —"

"Your plan's no good."

"You haven't even heard it yet!" Seth said, annoyed by his friend's impassivity.

"Doesn't matter," Ryan answered, his expression purposefully blank. He knew how much it bugged Seth and couldn't resist getting a little revenge for the groady toenail clippings all over his floor. "There not a chance in hell you're hooking up with Summer this weekend."

"That's where you're wrong, my friend," Seth said. "Once we put my awesome plan into effect —"

"We?" Ryan raised an eyebrow.

"Yes. You'll be distracting Marissa in the other room while Summer and I are making sweet love."

Ryan picked a pillow off the bed and threw it at Seth's head. Seth looked at him, outraged.

"What was that for?"

"Never use the expression 'making sweet love' again, okay?"

"I won't if you let me tell you my plan," Seth said.

Ryan sighed. "Fine."

Seth clapped his palms together. "All right!" he said. "All we need to do is make sure that the four of us are on the same team for the scavenger hunt. Then when we get to L.A., we decide, hey, why spend the extra time driving back and forth to Newport every night? Why not just get a hotel? So we do, and the rest is destiny." Seth smiled at Ryan and leaned back, waiting for the kudos to start rolling in. "Well? Whaddaya think?"

"That's the worst plan I've ever heard."

Seth blinked, an injured expression on his face. "You're just confused by its Machiavellian simplicity."

Ryan shook his head, exasperated. "There's no plan there! Just because you and Summer are in a hotel together, it doesn't mean anything is going to happen. You guys were in a hotel in San Diego together and nothing happened."

"Ah, but Summer was with Zach then. Now she's free, I'm free, and after spending an entire weekend with me, how will she be able to resist?"

"Do you want a list?"

"Ha ha." Seth made a face at Ryan. "Look, just help me figure out how to get us all on the same team, okay, and we'll figure the rest out as we go along."

"We could call the girls and tell them we want to partner up with them," Ryan suggested, but Seth shook his head.

"That's too obvious. We need to be subtle if this is going to work." Seth leaned closer to Ryan, and spoke in what he hoped was a very profound, insightful voice. "Think like the fox, and you'll get the chicks."

Ryan looked at Seth, his expression deadpan once more. "Yeah, now I'm not so sure *I* want to be on the same team with you."

"I think we should team up with Cohen and Ryan," Summer said. She and Marissa were hanging out in a booth in Ruby's Diner, scarfing down

7

cheeseburgers and going over the entry forms for the scavenger hunt.

The social committee had gone home after their spa day and started making phone calls, and before the week was out, every single student at Harbor, with the exception of a sophomore who was summering in Europe and a junior who was parked at Exeter's summer program until he brought his grades up enough to be considered for Stanford, had signed up.

Marissa and Summer were thrilled with the success of their idea, but they also had their hands full, with dozens of registration forms and checks made out to A Dream to Share. Everyone at Harbor seemed really into the idea of doing something for charity. The main attraction of the scavenger hunt, however, was the prospect of a parent-free weekend in Los Angeles.

All the kids spent the better part of the week deliberating where to book hotel rooms and which clubs had the most lax ID policies.

Equally riveting was the selection of teammates. The decision about which four people would make up a team was vital. The wrong mix of people and the weekend could be ruined, which was why Marissa raised a skeptical eyebrow at Summer's suggestion.

"Are you serious?" she asked. She snatched a french fry from Summer's plate and dipped it into a smudge of ketchup before popping it into her mouth. "You really want to spend the entire weekend with Seth?" she mumbled through a mouthful of potato.

"Well, I just thought that Ryan's probably really good at reading maps and figuring out clues and stuff," Summer said, purposely avoiding meeting Marissa's eyes. "I mean, we want to win the scavenger hunt, don't we?"

Marissa wasn't buying it, though. "Oh my god, you want to spend the weekend with Seth Cohen," she teased.

"I don't know," Summer admitted. "I mean, no, I don't want to . . . do anything with him. But it would be fun for the four of us to hang out together, don't you think?"

"Well," Marissa said, trying not to grin. "Ryan is really good with maps."

"Thanks," Summer said, then looked up, panic flashing across her face. "Oh, god, there they are. Be subtle, okay?"

Seth and Ryan had come into the diner. They looked around for a place to sit and, spotting the girls, came over and slid into their booth.

"Working on the scavenger hunt, I see," Seth said casually. He picked up a couple of entry forms and looked at the names. "Ooh, Stephany Folsom — I wouldn't want her on my team. Would you, Ryan?" He gave Ryan a pointed look — time to put the plan in action!

"Why, no, Seth, I wouldn't," Ryan answered, sighing. Seth always went through such machinations — Ryan still thought it'd be easier just to ask

9

the girls straight out. But when Seth Cohen had a plan, you had no choice but to follow.

"You need to be careful who you team up with," Summer said casually. "Coop and I were just trying to figure out who we wanted to be with."

Seth adopted a look of surprise. "Ryan and I were just doing the same thing! So you guys don't have partners, and we don't have part-ners — hmmm." He scratched his head, thinking hard.

"Huh," Summer said, her tone matching Seth's. "That's quite a coincidence."

"Isn't it?" Seth agreed.

Marissa's and Ryan's eyes met across the table.

"Hey, I have an idea!" Marissa said brightly, trying not to laugh. "Maybe the four of us could be a team!"

"What a good idea!" Ryan said, with a wide smile plastered on his face. "Let's do that."

Seth and Summer looked at each other and shrugged.

"I guess," Seth said. "If you guys want to."

"Sure, whatever," Summer said. "I really don't care. Anyway, I should get going."

"Me too," Marissa said. The boys stood up to let the girls slide out of the booth. "Guess we'll see you this weekend."

"Bye," Ryan said, and the girls walked away.

The second Marissa and Summer were outside, Summer clutched Marissa's arm. "Thank you so much!" she said.

"Anything to help you find true love," Marissa answered, laughing and ducking away from the swat Summer aimed at her.

Inside the diner, Seth was grinning triumphantly at Ryan.

"See?" he said. "Worked like magic."

Ryan nodded. "That was — pretty smooth."

"Thanks," Seth said, "And now? We need to start figuring out phase two of Operation Summer Lovin'. You want some coffee?"

"*Lots* of coffee," Ryan said wearily. This was going to be a *loooong* weekend.

THE

2

"Coffee," Seth croaked, groggily fumbling for the pot. He groped around the coffeemaker where it usually was — and came up empty. He let out a little whimper, blindly rubbing the sleep from his eyes . . . and spotted Ryan, pouring the last drops from the pot into his own mug.

"Please," Seth begged him, holding out his empty mug.

Ryan regarded him through sleep-heavy eyes. Seth summoned up his most pitiful expression, and Ryan finally relented, tipping half of the steaming coffee from his own cup into Seth's.

"Bless you," said Seth, cradling the cup in both hands and taking a long, soul-reviving sip. "I haven't been up this early since —"

"Since school ended!" Sandy boomed, appearing behind Ryan. He was fully dressed, in contrast to the boys, who were still in their pajamas. He beamed at Seth and Ryan, while busily measuring fresh beans into the grinder. He flipped it on — and the loud grinding noise made both boys cringe.

"I knew that'd wake you up," Sandy said, and tipped the grounds into a filter. As the coffee began brewing, he clapped Seth on the back. "Isn't this nice, all us men together again, greeting the morning with a big smile?"

"Yeah, right," Seth mumbled, taking another gulp of coffee.

Ryan covered a huge yawn with his hand, then grinned back at Sandy.

"There you go," Sandy told Ryan. "You guys excited about the big weekend?"

"I'll be more excited after the sun comes up," Seth grouched. "Remind me why we agreed to do this?"

"Because it's fun," Ryan told him. He pulled a bagel out of the toaster and dropped it on a plate, taking the carton of cream cheese Sandy handed him and fishing around in the silverware drawer for a knife.

"But why does it have to start so early? I'd like to ask A Dream to Share to make my dream of going back to bed come true," Seth complained. He grabbed the bag of bagels from the counter and started to rummage through it. Sandy and Ryan watched him with amused expressions.

"Are you planning on touching, like, every single one of them? Because I think you missed one near the bottom," Ryan told him.

"I can't find a cinnamon raisin one. I know there was one left — where is it?"

x

To answer, Ryan picked up his bagel and took a big crunching bite.

Seth yanked at his hair with his hands in frustration. "Tell me you're not eating the last cinnamon raisin bagel," he pleaded.

"You snooze, you lose," Ryan told him, and took another bite, licking the cream cheese off his lips with a blissful expression.

"How about letting me have half?" Seth asked with a hopeful smile.

"No way," Ryan told him. "I already gave you half of my coffee."

"Oh, come on! Give me half!" Seth lunged for the bagel, but Ryan was faster. He snatched up the other half of the bagel and gave it a big lick.

"Oh, very mature," Seth said.

"You still want it? Here, you can have it," Ryan teased, holding out the saliva-laden bagel to Seth.

"You think you're being funny, but you're the one who's going to have to sit next to me when my blood sugar drops and I get cranky," Seth informed him.

Ryan shot him a panicked look and grabbed the bakery bag. "There's got to be another cinnamon raisin one in here somewhere!" he exclaimed, rummaging through the bagels himself.

"Okay, you two," Sandy said, "if you don't get a move on it, we'll be late picking up the girls, and by the time we get to L.A., the hunt will be over."

"Better hurry, Seth," Ryan said. "If your plan is going to work, I think you're going to need every moment you can get with Summer."

Seth looked at him for a second, then turned and bolted toward his room. "I'll be ready in five minutes!" he shouted over his shoulder. "Dad! Go warm up the car!"

Marissa and Summer were waiting outside Caleb's house with a cardboard carrier tray of Starbucks when Sandy's car pulled up. They clambered into the backseat, passing out lattes to the three men.

"Ahhhh." Seth took a long, satisfying sip. "This weekend is off to a great start."

Marissa leaned forward and spoke to Sandy. "Thanks so much for driving us all the way to Los Angeles."

"My pleasure," Sandy said.

"Yeah, thanks," Summer added. "Although I still don't see why they wouldn't let us drive ourselves."

"A lot of the kids doing the scavenger hunt are under sixteen and don't have their licenses yet," Marissa explained. "It wouldn't be fair if some teams had cars and others didn't."

"But how are we supposed to get around?" Summer asked. "If we need to take taxis everywhere, then I need to stop at an ATM."

The other three kids exchanged a look. "Um, they gave everyone who registered a bus pass," Seth said. "Didn't they send you one?"

"They were serious?" Summer asked in disbelief. "I thought that was a joke. They can't honestly expect us to spend the weekend riding around on buses like some sort of — hoboes."

"Hoboes rode the rails, not buses," Sandy told her. "And it could be fun, getting in touch with the common people."

"If anyone tries to touch me, I'll mace him, common or not."

"Don't worry, Summer, I'll protect you," Seth said. He raised his eyebrows at Ryan — *See? The plan is working already!* — then gave Summer a reassuring pat on the arm. "I have lots of experience riding buses. I rode one up to Portland to visit Luke last summer, rode one home from San Diego after we pitched our comic last spring —"

"So basically you're saying that any time you have some big disaster in your life, you end up on a bus. Great," Summer said.

"Oh my god, you're right," Seth said. "I never thought of that. Buses have played a part in all the lowest points of my life. Dad? Can you give me money for taxis?"

"No."

Seth leaned back against the seat and let out a breath. "This weekend? Is doomed."

"Maybe this weekend will give you a chance to change your luck," Ryan told him. "After all, the bad things have always happened *before* you got on the bus, but we'll be on the bus in just a couple hours, and nothing bad has happened to you so far, right?"

Seth stared out the window, his face tragic. "Well, you did eat my bagel this morning," he said.

The other three kids looked at one another, then all smacked Seth at once.

"Ow!" he said, scrunching himself up against the door as far away from them as he could get and rubbing his arm. "See? It's already starting."

THE
3

The scavenger hunt was already starting when Sandy dropped the four kids at the kickoff point in Griffith Park. There were hundreds of kids milling around the wide grassy lawn, while grown-ups in VOLUNTEER T-shirts ran around shepherding groups of students to various registration tables. Summer and Marissa waved to some friends they knew from Harbor, and Liesl from the social committee came running up to them.

"Oh my god, you guys, this is so much fun," she said in a breathless voice. "Have you picked up your packet yet?"

Marissa shook her head. "We just got here."

"You have to pick up your packet!" Liesl bubbled. "I got mine at seven — I was the first one here! But don't worry — the list of clues is sealed, so the Hyenas didn't get a head start."

"The Hyenas?" Summer asked, wrinkling her nose.

"That's my team's name. The Harbor Hyenas.

You know, hyenas are the biggest scavengers of the animal kingdom. That's cute, right?"

"Sure," Marissa said nicely. But Summer was lost in thought.

"I didn't know we had to come up with a team name," she said.

"You don't *have* to," Liesl told her, "but everyone is. Well, I'm going to get back to my team. See you guys later!"

Liesl scampered away, and Ryan turned to the group. "Guess I better go pick up our packet." He walked away, toward the long tables where volunteers were signing teams in.

Marissa looked like she was about to go after him, when Summer turned to her.

"How about the Sassy Scavengers?" she said.

"What?" Marissa asked, but Seth was already shaking his head.

"Absolutely not. We need a team name that expresses both our coolness and our mad scavenging skills. Think big. Think mythical." He shut his eyes for a minute, his forehead screwed up in concentration, then snapped his fingers. "I got it: Team Shoshei."

"Team Sushi?" Summer repeated, with a chance-in-hell sneer.

"Shoshei," Seth corrected her. "They're a band of godlike warriors from *Wolverine Soultaker 3*."

"Veto," Summer said.

Seth blinked. "Wait. You don't get to veto."

19

"Yes, I do," said Summer. "Team Shiny?"

"Veto," Seth shot back at her. "Squadron Supreme?"

"Is that another comic?" Summer asked, her hands on her hips.

"Yes, but it's a really cool one."

"No comics!" Summer said. "You know how bad things turned out last time we collaborated on a comic."

"I guess," Seth admitted. They stood silently for a second, thinking, then Summer made another suggestion.

"Princess Sparkle's Hunting Heroes?"

"Not bad," Seth said, "but a bit of a mouthful. What about Team Sparkle Motion? Get a little *Donnie Darko*-Princess Sparkle combo?"

"I love it!" Summer said, and threw her arms open, addressing the clusters of kids milling about nearby. "Look out, L.A., Team Sparkle Motion has arrived."

"*We're* Team Sparkle Motion," said a chubby kid in a Dragonball Z T-shirt. "We picked it days ago."

"Damn," Seth muttered, "that's such a good name. Um, Team Dragonball Z?"

"Enough!" Marissa shouted. Seth and Summer turned to her in surprise as she ranted at them. "I cannot listen to another second of this! I've had it."

"We're just trying to come up with a good name," Summer said, subdued.

"Let's just use our initials or something and be done with it," Marissa commanded.

"Summer, Marissa, Ryan, Seth. S, M, R, S." Seth sounded the letters out. "Smears. Huh. It's different. But kind of catchy. Team Smears."

"Fine," Marissa said, over Summer's protests. "If it'll get you guys to stop arguing, we're the Smears."

Ryan came walking back to them, carrying a plastic bag with the A Dream to Share logo on it. "I got our packet," he told the group.

Seth gave him a big smile. "Guess what? Our team's name is the Smears! Pretty punk rock, huh? I bet Sid Vicious would name his team the Smears."

"Somehow I doubt that Sid Vicious did a lot of charity scavenger hunts," Ryan said.

"But if he did — ?" Seth prompted.

Ryan was spared having to answer by the appearance of a quartet of kids who came sauntering up to them. The two giant, oafish guys were both wearing letter jackets that said DEL VISTA FOOTBALL across the back, and that spelled trouble.

Del Vista was Harbor's biggest rival, and Ryan had had a run-in with some Del Vista players when he first moved to the O.C. He was not eager to start their weekend off with a fistfight, but the jocks weren't the ones starting trouble — it was the pretty, petite cheerleaders who were with them.

"I guess they're letting *anyone* into this scavenger hunt," a blond cheerleader said bitchily. "I thought the A Dream to Share foundation would have held to higher standards."

"Oh, right, Autumn, all those cancer victims are

really elitist about where their funding comes from," Summer retorted.

Ryan caught Marissa's eye. *Autumn?* he mouthed silently at her.

Marissa nodded and rolled her eyes.

"Better a cancer victim than a fashion victim," Autumn replied, giving Summer's Missoni sundress a disparaging look.

"That's nice," Summer said. "That shows a lot of class."

Seth, guided by some suicidal chivalrous impulse, decided it would be a good idea to get involved. "Speaking of fashion victim —" he said, and seven sets of eyes turned to him. "Are you kidding, wearing those jackets?"

The players both took a menacing step toward him, so Seth did some quick verbal backtracking, holding his hands out to placate them.

"I just meant, it's, like, eighty degrees out. Aren't you hot?"

"Shut up, loser," one football dude grunted, and the other laughed and held his hand up for a quick high five.

"Well, it's good to see that the heat hasn't affected that rapier wit," Seth said, and Ryan, sensing the potential for this to turn ugly, put out a hand and tugged the back of Seth's shirt. He pulled Seth away from the Del Vista guys, then spoke to them in a soft, unsmiling voice.

"Why don't you guys go your way and we'll go ours, and we'll see you at the finish line."

"If you make it to the finish line," the first football dude said.

The second player laughed and chucked his buddy on the shoulder. "Yeah, if you losers can even find the finish line."

The football players clomped away, and Autumn and her friend turned to follow.

"Good luck," she said to Summer. "You're going to need it."

The gang from Harbor watched the Del Vista students disappear into the crowd of kids milling about, then Summer stamped her foot in disgust.

"I *hate* that Autumn Cabot," she said. "We were in twirl camp together when we were eight, and the coach always made us be partners because she thought it was cute that we were both seasons. But she was a bitch then, and she's a bitch now."

"Wait — twirl camp? What exactly is twirl camp?" Seth asked her.

"We learned to twirl batons," Summer said, as if it couldn't be more obvious. "I was supposed to twirl the fire batons in the end-of-camp show, but Autumn was afraid of them, so since I was stuck with her as a partner, they let Liz Hulings twirl them instead."

Summer looked put out at the memory, but Seth was gazing at her with a dreamy expression. "My god, you and fire batons. This is going to take my fantasy life to a whole new level."

"Ew! Cohen!" Summer said, giving him another smack.

"God, stop hitting me," Seth told her. "I'm all bruised."

Ryan cocked an eyebrow at Marissa. "Were you a twirler, too?"

"No, that was exclusively Summer's domain," she told him. "I spent all my time when I was eight trying to get my parents to trade Kaitlin in for a puppy."

They shared a smile, and Ryan was the first to look away, glancing down at his watch. "When are they going to get this thing on the road?" he asked.

As if they'd heard him, a jolly-looking gray-haired woman in a pantsuit tapped on a microphone that was set up by the registration tables and addressed the crowd.

"Hello, everyone, and thank you for taking part in the A Dream to Share Foundation's first annual Los Angeles scavenger hunt weekend."

The kids all clapped and cheered, and the woman's grin stretched wider, making her look even more jovial.

"I know you're all eager to get out there and start hunting, so I'll be brief. Each team has been given a sealed envelope with a list of clues inside, which will lead you to ten exciting and unexpected places in and around Los Angeles. You need to solve the clues, go to the locations, and bring back a picture or a souvenir. On Sunday, whichever team gets to our finish line at the Magic Tower first —"

She paused here, while the kids let out another cheer at the news that the finish line would be at the amusement park.

When the noise died down, she leaned back into the mic. "Whoever solves all ten clues and makes it to Magic Tower first will be the winner, but I promise you that every one of you is going to have a great time. Now, there are three rules that you all must follow. Number one: No cars. I don't care if you bus, bike, or blade it, but you have to get yourself to each location without driving — and no cabs!

"Number two: Nothing illegal! We want everyone to arrive at the finish line safe and sound on Sunday. And the third rule? Have fun!"

The kids applauded for a third time, and this time the woman didn't wait for them to quiet down before continuing. She shouted into the microphone over their clapping, "Okay, scavengers, on your marks, get set, go!"

The park erupted as kids shouted to their friends, running for the bus and tearing open their envelopes. Seth, Ryan, Marissa, and Summer watched, amused, as Liesl ran past, shrieking and yipping like a hyena. When the mayhem finally died down and most of the kids had cleared out of the park, Seth turned to the others.

"So, I saw a coffee place down on Franklin when we were driving here. You guys want to grab another cup while we figure out these clues?"

"Sounds good," Ryan said, and Marissa and Summer nodded.

"Look out, L.A.," Summer said as they started walking down the street away from the park, "here come the Smears."

4

Fifteen minutes later, they were seated at a side-walk table at a coffee shop called the Bourgeois Pig, and Seth finally had a cinnamon raisin bagel in front of him. He smeared cream cheese over one half, then crammed practically the whole thing into his mouth.

"God, Cohen, nice table manners," Summer said. She hitched her chair a fraction of an inch away from his.

"Sorry, but I'm starving," Seth mumbled, spray-ing crumbs. He held up a finger for them to wait while he finished chewing, then he swallowed and spoke in his normal voice. "Sorry," he repeated. "Now, let's open this bad boy up and win this game."

"Okay." Ryan put the plastic bag he'd gotten at registration on the table and started pulling things out of it. "Two Polaroid cameras. Map of L.A. A Dream to Share decorative patch — here you go," he said, handing the scrap of fabric to Summer.

"Gee, thanks," she said, tucking it into her

purse. "Next time I wear my old Girl Scout uniform I'll be sure to sew this onto the sash."

"Summer in a Girl Scout uniform," Seth said longingly. "New fantasy number two."

The other kids burst out laughing, and Summer wrinkled her nose at him. "I'd hit you again, but I know you're delicate."

Seth nodded. "Like a ripe pear."

"Why don't we check out the rest of this packet," Ryan said. He pulled out a bunch of folded pamphlets and spread them on the table. "Let's see. Um —"

"Those are bus schedules." Ryan looked over to the next table, at the person who had spoken. It was a boy, maybe ten years old, tops, who was sitting with three friends, drinking apple juice and sifting through the same papers as Ryan.

"Hey, are you guys doing this scavenger hunt, too?" Summer asked them.

"Yeah," the boy replied. "We're Team Gummi Worms."

The Harbor kids exchanged a glance. "I thought you had to be in high school to take part," Marissa said.

"We are. Kind of," the boy answered. His friends started laughing, and he grinned at Marissa. "We take advanced math at Calabasas Prep, so they said that counted."

"Cool," Marissa said. "So what grade are you really in?"

"Sixth."

Ryan cocked an eyebrow. "And your parents are letting you go all over the city by yourselves?"

"Uh-uh." The kid shook his head and sucked some juice up through his straw. "My mom's going to follow the bus in her car."

His friend, a runty little redhead covered with freckles, piped up. "Have you looked at the clues yet? They're really hard."

"Yeah, we haven't gotten any of them yet," the first kid added.

"Well, I'm sure you'll figure them all out," Marissa told him. "Good luck."

"Thanks." The kid turned back to his own table and blew bubbles into his orange juice through the straw. His friends all started blowing bubbles, too, and the Harbor kids laughed.

"All right, let's get crackin'," Ryan said, ripping open the envelope with the clues. "After all, we don't want to be beaten by a bunch of ten-year-olds."

"We're eleven!" the kid shouted, and his table erupted in giggles.

Ryan rolled his eyes and shifted around so he was facing away from the table of sixth graders. "Okay, here we go. Clue number one—" He unfolded the paper. "'Go for a ride where angels take flight.'" He put the paper down and looked blankly at the other kids. They stared back at him, equally at a loss.

"Okay. Where do angels take flight? Clouds? Heaven?"

29

"Los Angeles means 'the angels,'" Marissa said. "Maybe we're supposed to go to the airport."

"Huh. Maybe."

The kids thought about it some more.

"That organizer lady said we'd be going to exciting, unexpected places. Is the airport really unexpected?" Summer asked.

"I wasn't expecting it," Ryan said.

"The arcade in the United Terminal has *Dance Dance Revolution*," Seth said. "That's . . . exciting, maybe."

"I don't know," Ryan said. "Why don't we skip this one for now and come back to it later?"

The other kids nodded, and Ryan read the next clue. "'Go to the valley and take a picture of the bridges.'"

They sat in silence for a minute, thinking, then Marissa said, "Moving on?"

"Please," Seth said. "What's number three?"

"'Come face-to-face with a dragon.'"

"All right, that's more like it. We can do this," Seth said. "Dragons are big lizards that breathe fire and fly. So if we wanted to find one . . . where would we go?" He trailed off, but then —

"Wait a minute!" The red-haired kid at the next table had been listening in on Seth's conversation, and now he jumped up from his seat, excited, and whispered something into his friends' ears.

"Yeah! That's it! We got one!" The sixth graders hollered and scrambled up from their table. In a flash they were headed down the street toward the bus stop, trailed by a middle-aged woman in a station wagon.

Seth looked at the others, disbelief spreading across his face. "Great. They got one. The ten-year-olds got one. We're being beaten by Team Gummi Worms."

"They *are* in advanced math," Summer said consolingly. "Besides, we're only on number three. Read us number four, Ryan."

Ryan looked down at the paper. "Count the pigs on Vernon Avenue. All right!" He dropped the clue list and picked up the map.

"Do you know what that means?" Marissa asked him, surprised.

"Nope," Ryan said, his head buried in the map. "But — I've found Vernon Avenue. I vote that we go there and start looking for anything that's pink and oinks."

"Sounds good," Seth said. He picked up a bus schedule and looked over Ryan's shoulder at the map. "Where's Vernon Ave.?"

"In Watts," Ryan said. "So I bet if we caught a downtown bus —"

"Wait a minute," Summer said. "Watts? We're not going to Watts. They have riots in Watts."

"Yeah, like fifteen years ago," Seth said. "I'm sure it's perfectly safe now."

"Oh, you're sure?" Summer said. "Your highly evolved sense of street smarts is telling you that Watts is a big ole tourist attraction now?"

"Hey, I know the streets," Seth protested. "I've

31

been to —" He tried to think up an example that would make him sound tough. "I've been in *alleys*."

Marissa put a reassuring hand on Summer's arm. "The people who organized the scavenger hunt wouldn't send us somewhere dangerous," she said.

"But *Watts*? Come on, Coop. This weekend was supposed to be about having fun, not traipsing around gangland on some nasty public bus."

"It could be fun," Marissa said uncertainly.

"No," Summer insisted, "it's going to be smelly and dangerous. Besides, do you really want to risk Seth's bad bus mojo? We'll probably get lost and end up in the middle of a knife fight."

"I thought you said this weekend was going to change my bus-riding karma," Seth protested.

"Oh, please," Summer told him. "If we get on a bus with you, we'll be dead by lunchtime."

The kids looked at one another, dejected and unsure what to do next, when all of a sudden a car driving along Franklin slowed down in front of the café and the person in the backseat rolled down the window.

Autumn Cabot was inside, and as the car passed the table where the kids were sitting, she leaned her head out and shouted, "Have fun riding the bus, losers!"

With a squeal of tires, the car sped up, and as it raced down the street, the last thing the kids could see was the driver sticking his meaty football-player fist out the window and giving them all the finger.

"Hey, they're cheating," Seth said. "They're not allowed to drive. That's totally unfair."

Summer rose to her feet, staring after her rival until the car was out of sight, her mouth set in an angry, determined line. "I'll show her who the losers are. Cohen! What time's the next bus?"

Seth hurriedly scanned the schedule he was still clutching. "Um, there's one due in five minutes a block from here."

"So what are you people waiting for?" Summer said. "Let's go! We've got pigs to count!"

The other kids jumped up, gathering up their things.

"So you don't mind taking your life into your hands by getting on a bus with me?" Seth asked.

"If it meant showing up Autumn Cabot," Summer told him, "I'd drive the damn thing myself."

THE OC

5

"Ew, ew, ew," Summer whispered under her breath. She was squeezed into a window seat on the number fourteen bus and was not happy. The enormous man next to her, wearing only a tank top and a miniscule pair of gym shorts, was sweating so profusely that every time the bus jostled and part of him touched part of Summer, it left a wet splotch on her dress.

Making things worse, the woman in front of her had such prodigious amounts of hair that it hung over the back of her seat, rippling down practically into Summer's lap.

Summer was almost praying for Cohen's curse to strike — even death would be preferable to this. And what in the world was that smell? Didn't people believe in deodorant anymore?

Seth was sitting catty-cornered to her, in the seat behind Marissa and Ryan. He kept making little hand gestures, offering to switch places with her, but extricating herself from around her seatmate without touching any more of him than she already had would require Herculean effort, and Summer just wasn't up for it. Besides, it would be rude to be obvious about how completely icky she found these people, and she didn't want to hurt anyone's feelings.

After what felt like hours, the man next to her closed his newspaper and stuffed it into his backpack, preparing to disembark. He reached across Summer to ring the sensor strip to alert the driver to stop, and Summer froze in horror as his reeking, wet, matted, bare armpit was shoved practically into her face. She was so disturbed she couldn't even repeat her customary "ew," but just gave a little squeak of dismay.

Finally the bus groaned to a stop and the instant the man got off, Summer hurled herself from the hell seat.

"Oh. My. God. Did you see that?" she asked, her entire body contorting in disgust.

"Are you kidding? It looked like you were being attacked by a grizzly," Seth said.

Ryan and Marissa turned around in their seat so they were facing their friends. "At least you know it can't get any worse than that," Marissa told her. "You've seen rock bottom, so all your future bus trips will seem great in comparison to this one."

Summer gave another shudder, then squeezed herself next to Seth on his seat. "I'm not going back there," she said, swinging her eyes back to the newly vacated seat. "I swear to god, he left puddles of sweat on the seat."

"You sit here with me. There's plenty of room," Seth told Summer, earning an evil look from the woman sitting on Seth's other side. She pushed her way into the aisle and headed toward the back of the bus, and Seth slid over to give Summer more room.

A couple of tween girls boarded the bus and piled into the seat Summer had been sitting in, chattering loudly.

"Oh my god, Grady is so cute, I love him," one of the girls said. She had on bright pink lipstick and was clutching a teen fanzine with the cast of *The Valley* on the cover.

"I love him, too. I worship him," the second girl said. She had her hair in two messy braids, which would have been cute if she weren't chewing on the end of one. "I can't believe we're going to meet him. I'm going to have them take my picture with him, and right when they take it, I'm going to kiss him!"

"Well, I'm totally going to ask him out," Lipstick declared.

"Shut up, you are not," Braids said.

"Yah-huh. I'm going to walk right up to him and say, 'Grady Bridges, you are my destiny,' and he's going to dump that nasty hag April and marry me instead."

The girls burst out laughing, and Summer leaned over to them. "Are you guys talking about *The Valley*?" she asked.

36

The girls stopped laughing and regarded Summer suspiciously. "So?" Lipstick said.

"It's my favorite show, too," Summer told them. Then, unable to resist, "I know Grady Bridges. I went to a party with him once."

"Well, pin a rose on you," Braids snotted. "We're meeting him this Sunday."

"Yeah?" Summer said, skepticism heavy in her voice. "Where?"

"The whole cast is going to be at the Encino Tower Records," Lipstick said. "Now, can you please MYOB?"

The girls went back to their conversation, and Summer turned to her friends, an idea sparking in her eyes.

"God, what is it with the preteens in Los Angeles?" Marissa said, glaring at the giggling tweens. "First those brats at the coffee shop, now these little monsters?"

"Oh, 'cause all the junior high kids in Orange County are so mature and respectful," Seth said.

Before Marissa could retort, however, Summer grabbed her arm, a huge smile spreading across her face. "What was that second clue again?" she asked.

"Uh, come face-to-face with a dragon," Ryan said, but Summer shook her head.

"No, the one about the bridges," she said, and Ryan fished the paper out of his pocket.

"Go to the valley and take a picture of the bridges," he read.

"Grady Bridges is the star of *The Valley*," Summer said. "He's doing a public appearance in the real Valley this weekend, where people can take his picture."

"Oh my god, you figured it out!" Marissa squealed, throwing her arms around Summer.

"And here's something even better — we don't need to wait until Sunday to get the picture."

"We don't?"

"What's the point of being friends with a TV star if you can't just drop by the set and take your picture with him whenever you want?"

Ryan darted his eyes at Seth. "Ah . . . you're friends with Grady?" he asked Summer.

"Well, he knows me. I bet he'd be glad to see me."

"You know, you're right," Seth said. "Why don't we split up, and you and me can go to wherever it is that they shoot *The Valley* —"

"Burbank," Summer told him.

"*Burbank*," Seth repeated. "Right. And while we're dropping in on our friend Grady, Ryan and Marissa can go take care of this pig thing, and that way we'll kill two birds with one stone."

"Um." Marissa looked back and forth from Seth to Ryan. "I'd actually kind of like to see a real TV studio."

"Okay, so . . . what? We'll all go to *The Valley* set after we finish up in Compton."

"Watts," Ryan reminded him.

"Watts. Yes." Now it was Seth's turn to

ping-pong from one face to the other. "So — whaddaya think?"

"No, you were right, we should split up," Summer said. "The faster we solve these clues, the faster I can rub Autumn's face in it."

"Ah, the spirit of charity," Seth said. "It warms the heart." He rummaged in his jeans pocket for the bus schedule, which he carefully perused. "Well, if you ladies are going to Burbank, it appears that you are on the wrong bus."

"Maybe if we asked the driver to drop us in Burbank —" Summer started, and looked a little startled when Seth and Ryan burst out laughing.

"Actually? If you get off up here on Rimpau Avenue, a number 712 bus should be along in about three minutes that will drop you practically at the studio's doorstep," Seth told her, folding up the schedule and stuffing it back in his pocket.

"Not that the driver wouldn't be thrilled to pieces to revise his route for you," Ryan dead-panned.

"Ha-ha," Summer flatly told Ryan, then turned to Seth. "You're pretty good at this stuff," she said.

Seth blinked. "Wow. I mean, Summer . . . I don't know what to say you're finally recognizing my organizational —" He stopped short, as under-standing struck him. "Oh. You're talking about reading the schedule. Right."

A blush crept over his cheeks as he saw the other kids biting their lips to keep from laughing.

"Get off the bus," he told the girls, punching the sensor to get the driver to stop.

"We'll see you — and your schedule — later," Marissa said, and, as the bus lurched to a stop, the girls got up and left the boys to go count pigs by themselves.

"Bye," Seth called after them.

And as the doors shut behind them and the bus continued on its path toward Vernon Avenue, he leaned back in his seat, folding his arms behind his head and gazing at Ryan with a satisfied expression on his face.

"What are you looking so happy about?" Ryan asked him.

"The plan? Like clockwork, my friend. Learn from the master."

"The plan to make Summer fall for you by spending all your time together this weekend?"

"Yep."

Ryan looked around, puzzled. "Seems to me that you managed to get her to go off alone to see another guy."

Seth unfolded his arms and straightened up in his seat. "Okay," he said, the wheels turning, "the plan needs work."

"Maybe just a little," Ryan agreed.

"Well, we've got" — Seth looked out the window to glimpse a passing street sign — "forty blocks till we get to Vernon Avenue. Let's get that brainstorming action going. How do we get Summer to want me?"

"You could . . . punch out Autumn Cabot," Ryan suggested.

"True," Seth conceded. "I'd considered that. Only . . ."

"What if she hits back?" Ryan asked, finishing the thought.

"Like a ripe pear," Seth repeated, nodding.

"Then I guess we need to brainstorm some more," Ryan said.

And the two boys looked out the windows, lost in thought, as the bus continued down the street.

THE

6

"Ouch! Son of a . . ." Summer exclaimed as the mascara wand poked her in the eye for the third time.

She wiped the black smudge away with a finger and leaned closer to the bus window, using its reflection as a makeshift mirror. She carefully brushed the wand across her eyelashes and then, satisfied, put the mascara away and pulled out a lipstick. She puckered up, brought the tube to her lips . . . and the bus lurched, turning a corner and jostling her hand.

The lipstick skidded across her face, leaving a berry-colored streak on her cheek. "Damn it!" Summer said in frustration. She rummaged in her purse for a Kleenex and glared at Marissa, who was biting her lip to keep from laughing at her friend's predicament.

"Oh, so you think this is funny?" Summer asked, and Marissa nodded.

"Kind of," Marissa admitted. "You've got sort of a Marilyn Manson thing going on."

"I can't help it," Summer complained. "If this

stupid bus would try to go five seconds without hitting a pothole, maybe I could put my makeup on right."

"Why don't you wait until we get off the bus and do it then?" Marissa asked.

"Because then we will be at the studio, and I don't want Grady to see me looking all sweaty and gross. It's bad enough that I'm wearing these tacky shoes," Summer said, lifting her foot in the air and waggling it from side to side to show Marissa her Miu Miu slides.

"First of all, you don't look gross, you look great. And second, you love those shoes and they match your dress."

"But they're flats," Summer said, wrinkling her nose in distaste. "My legs look so much better in heels."

"But then you'd have to traipse all over the city in shoes you can't even walk in," Marissa consoled her. "Besides, I'm sure Grady won't even notice what you have on your feet."

"You think so?" Summer asked, hope in her voice.

Marissa nodded. "Yeah. He'll be too busy staring at the eyeliner all over your face."

And she cracked up as Summer wailed and started scrubbing off her makeup.

Finally the bus pulled up outside the studio, and Marissa and Summer clambered off.

"Well?" Marissa asked, looking around as the bus pulled away.

"Well what?" Summer asked back, bending down to inspect her face in the side mirror of a parked car. She wet a finger and rubbed away a last stray smudge under her eye.

"Where's Grady?"

"He's not going to be outside waiting for us," Summer said, in a don't-be-ridiculous voice. "He's probably on a soundstage or in his trailer or something."

"I *know* he's not out here waiting," Marissa answered, mimicking Summer's tone. "But this is a huge studio. How do we find him?"

"Oh." Summer looked at Marissa doubtfully. "You're right. Well, let's just go in and ask someone."

The two girls started toward the studio entrance — a huge gate with a bustling security booth. Cars were lined up in front of it, and guards were looking in everybody's trunk and checking underneath the cars with mirrors on long poles before they let anybody in.

Marissa and Summer walked up the narrow sidewalk and nonchalantly passed by the guard booth. Before they got a step farther, though, a massive man wearing mirror sunglasses and a uniform stepped in front of them, blocking their path.

"Excuse us," Summer said with a smile, trying to slip past him. But the guard folded his arms across his chest, giving them no room to get around him.

"Can I help you girls?" he asked.

44

"We're here to see Grady Bridges," Marissa said. "Can you tell us where to find him?"

The guard held out one meaty paw. "IDs?"

Summer and Marissa shared a glance — maybe this was going to work! They fished in their purses and handed the guard their driver's licenses.

Without a word, he stepped into the booth, pulling the door shut behind him.

Marissa and Summer waited for what seemed like hours while the guard was in the booth with their IDs.

"What could be taking so long?" Marissa whispered.

"Maybe Grady's in the middle of a scene and they can't reach him," Summer said. She shifted from foot to foot, bored. "It's so hot. I'm getting a sunburn."

"I have sunscreen, if you want it," Marissa said.

"All I want is to go inside," Summer said. Unable to stand waiting any longer, she leaned over and knocked on the window of the security booth. The guard glanced up at her, then returned his attention to his computer.

Impatient, Summer knocked again. This time the guard got up. He opened the door just a crack, but Summer could feel the blissfully cool air-conditioning stream out around him.

"Yes?" he asked.

"Uh, you have our IDs?" Summer reminded him. "And we're here to see Grady?"

"Right." The guard handed Summer both

licenses, then stepped out of the booth. "You weren't on the list, and nobody from *The Valley* is expecting you."

"We could have told you that an hour ago," Summer said, exasperated. "Grady doesn't know we're coming — it's a surprise visit."

"I can't let you on the lot," the guard said flatly. "Not unless you're on the list."

"But she knows him," Marissa said. "We went to a party with Grady once."

"I watched dailies in his Escalade," Summer bragged.

"And I drank tea with Prince Charles," the guard answered. "Now I need to ask you to turn around and go home."

"But we *do* know him," Summer insisted. "He'll be happy to see us."

"Not going to happen, ladies," the guard informed them. "Do I need to escort you off the property?"

"No," Marissa said, grabbing Summer's arm as she was about to argue. "Thanks anyway."

Marissa pulled Summer away from the guard. When they were out of earshot, she let go of Summer's arm.

"What a jerk," Summer said, scowling.

"Come on, there's got to be a back door or something," Marissa said. And the two girls started hiking around the perimeter of the huge studio lot. By the time they'd gotten most of the way around, Summer was very happy that she'd worn flats after

46

all, and was considering downgrading to sneakers next. The only other entrances they saw were guarded by gates and guards just like the front, but they did notice a line of people standing off to the side by the back gate.

The girls walked over and struck up a conversation with one of the people in line, a twenty-something woman with stringy hair and an oversized Lakers jacket.

"What's this line for?" Marissa asked.

"It's to be in the audience for *The Pat Diamond Show*," the woman answered.

"No way!" Marissa said, impressed. "I love that show. It's so trashy."

Pat Diamond was the host of a talk show that specialized in sordid sex scandals and freaks of nature. The guests tended to be people who wanted to legally marry their pets, or Siamese twins who were cheating with each other's husbands, or geriatric lingerie models. It was completely hilarious and tragic, and Marissa watched it every chance she could.

"They only let fifty people in," the stringy-haired woman told them. "I'm not sure if you're going to make it."

"We're not here for—" Summer started, but Marissa cut her off again.

"I hope we get in," she said. "We came all the way out here for this."

A young man wearing a headset and shorts appeared through a metal doorway and began ushering the line inside. As they moved forward with the line, Summer gave Marissa a little pinch.

"Coop! What are you doing? We don't have time for this."

"It'll get us inside," Marissa said. "And then we can go find Grady."

They reached the front of the line and the man touched each of them on the shoulder as they walked past him. ". . . Forty-four, forty-five . . ."

They walked down the hall with the rest of the crowd, and spotted a ladies' room door off to one side. Summer ducked inside, but as Marissa was about to follow her, a hand clamped down on her shoulder.

It was the young man with the headset. "There's a restroom on the set," he said. "But I need to keep you all together until we get there."

Marissa hesitated for a second. How was she going to let Summer know what happened to her? "OKAY, I'LL USE THE BATHROOM ON THE SET," she shouted, in a voice she hoped was loud enough for Summer to hear. The headset guy looked at her strangely, but she just smiled and shrugged. "Getting ready to shout at the show's guests," she told him in a normal volume. "Do you know what the topic is today?"

The guy consulted his clipboard. "Hoggies. People who get turned on by wallowing in mud."

"That's sick," Marissa said. "Let's go."

7

"I don't see any pigs," Seth told Ryan. They were standing on Vernon Avenue, a completely normal city street with businesses, restaurants, and not a single farm animal in sight. "Are you sure this is the right Vernon Avenue?"

"It's the only one on the map," Ryan answered, scanning the storefronts around him for any hint of the clue's meaning.

"You don't think —" Seth lowered his voice as a pair of heavyset old men walked past them. "You don't think when they said pigs they meant people who eat a lot?"

Ryan gave Seth a level look. "You eat a lot. Should I take your picture?"

"You might have to, since there are no pigs on this street."

"Let's walk up to the next block," Ryan said, not ready to admit defeat so quickly. "Maybe there's a pet store or something."

They started up the street, when Seth noticed a

sign jutting out from a doorway far ahead of them. "Does that say something about farms?" he asked, squinting.

Ryan gave it a look. "Farmer John's," he read, then gave Seth a sideways glance. "When was the last time you got your eyes checked?"

"Why?"

"You couldn't read that sign? That's really bad. Maybe there's something wrong with your vision."

"My eyes are fine."

"No, seriously, maybe you need glasses."

"I can see great," Seth insisted. "I don't need glasses. Besides, I was the one who saw the sign in the first place."

"Okay, okay," Ryan said as they walked toward Farmer John's. "But I think you'd look good in glasses. You'd look like Jeff Goldblum."

Seth perked up a bit. "Jeff Goldblum in *The Fly*? He was pretty cool back then."

"Yeah, I was thinking more Jeff Goldblum in those computer commercials."

"That Jeff Goldblum sucks," Seth said. "But it's beside the point, because I don't need glasses. 'Farmer John's. Family Owned Since 1931,'" he read. "See?"

"Yeah, now that we're standing right in front of it," Ryan said dryly. "Anyway, what is this? A butcher's?"

"Oh my god," Seth said, realizing. "It's a slaughterhouse. What sort of sick bastards at A Dream to

Share thought it would be fun to send us here to count pigs as they're sent off to die?"

"Wait —" Ryan took a step back and gazed down the street at the side of the endless Farmer John's building. "*That's* what we're counting."

Seth followed his gaze. Painted on the side of the building were a series of murals, all depicting pastoral farm scenes. Dozens and dozens of painted pigs cavorted through the murals, all the way down the block.

"We're supposed to count all of them?" Seth asked. "There must be a hundred."

"I'm up to fourteen already," Ryan answered, scanning the wall.

"I guess I'll start at the other end and meet you in the middle," Seth said, but Ryan was up to twenty-two and wasn't listening.

Seth wandered down to the other end of the block to begin counting the pigs there. The murals were pretty cool, actually. The pigs looked real, grazing or sleeping or wallowing in the mud. Not cartoons. Seth always thought there was something sort of creepy and upsetting about cute cartoon animals advertising restaurants or stores where the real animals were dead and being eaten. But these pigs were more "Circle of Life." As soon as he thought this, Seth was glad Ryan was half a block away. Otherwise he might have said it out loud, and then Ryan would make fun of him for the rest of the trip.

But it is *"Circle of Life,"* Seth told himself defensively. Then he stopped in front of the very last mural and began counting.

He was three murals down, and trying to decide whether or not the curly pink tail poking into the edge of the admittedly hot picture of the farmer's daughter should count as pig number fifty-seven, when a screech of tires made him look up.

A champagne-colored Mercedes slammed to a halt in front of the mural, and Seth realized with a sinking feeling that he recognized that car. It belonged to the lame-brain football jocks from Del Vista.

As if on cue, they tumbled out, followed by Autumn and her friend. The football players had discarded their jackets, and their huge biceps bulged threateningly out of their muscle tees as they sauntered over to Seth.

"Look, it's that geek from this morning," the first player bellowed.

His friend laughed and stuck his face right up next to Seth's. "Nineteen. Twenty-eight. Forty-six. Thirty-one. Eighty-seven. Fifty-nine. Forty two . . ." he chanted.

"Very mature," Seth told him. "Trying to make me lose count. I used to do that in the second grade."

"Eighty-one. Seventy-two. Forty-three. Twelve . . ." the second football player chimed in.

Seth sighed. Where was Ryan and his temper when he needed them? He shot a look down the block — Ryan was engrossed in his counting and hadn't even noticed the Del Vista kids' arrival. Seth was going to have to handle this on his own. "Listen" — he searched for a name — "Brutus —"

The players looked confused. "Who's Brutus?"

"Or whatever your names are."

"I'm Chaz," the dumber one said. "That's Mickey."

"Well, listen, Chaz and Mickey, we clearly got off on the wrong foot. But why so hostile? I see you took my advice about the jackets. You're a lot more comfortable now, aren't you? You don't have to thank me," he said modestly, but Chaz didn't seem thankful.

"Shut up about my jacket," Chaz said. "Just 'cause you're never gonna letter in anything."

"Maybe he could letter in band," Mickey said. "Or, uh . . ." He trailed off, unable to think up another example.

"Debate?" Seth suggested. "Chess club? Come on, Mickey, if you're going to make the joke, then *make the joke*."

Mickey blinked, completely disarmed by Seth's bravado. Before his sluggish synapses could rally a response from his brain to his mouth, however, Autumn shouted to him from in front of the first mural. "Mickey! Chaz! Get over here and help us count."

The jocks dutifully turned and trotted away, and Seth watched them go with a sneer on his face. "I'm surprised you even know how to count," he muttered under his breath, then turned back to the mural. Okay, that curly pink tail was number —

Damn it! The jocks' technique had worked and Seth had lost count. He groaned in frustration. "One, two, three . . . ," he began, standing in front of the first mural again.

THE OC

8

"Nineteen. Twenty. Twenty-one . . ." Summer counted off the stages as she passed each one.

She had hidden in the bathroom for five minutes after she heard Marissa's shout, making use of the time to repair her butchered makeup job, then slipped out the door and onto the lot.

A cute P.A. on a bicycle stopped to ask if she was lost, and when she said she was looking for Grady, he mistook her for an extra and pointed the way to stage twenty-four, where the cameras were rolling on the set of *The Valley*.

Summer was so excited that she practically skipped down the path to the stage, but the closer she got to the set, the slower she went, until now, with the big green 24 that was painted on the side of the soundstage in sight, she was walking so slowly she might as well be standing still. She told herself it was so she wouldn't look all sweaty when she saw him, but in truth, there was another reason Summer was putting off her arrival at her destination.

It had been over a year and a half since she'd gone to that party with Grady, and as much as she hated to admit it, to herself or anyone else, things hadn't gone so well between the two of them. Summer had been so obsessed with Cohen that when Grady had tried to kiss her, she pushed him away. Summer honestly wasn't too sure that Grady would remember her at all, but if he did, she was pretty sure he'd remember that.

Well, maybe it won't be a problem, she told herself. Grady had probably kissed hundreds of girls in the backseat of that truck. What difference would one little rejection make? Besides, she and Cohen ended up dating for months after that night — so she had a good reason for not wanting to kiss anyone else. Grady would understand.

Although thinking this through made her think about Cohen, and then she really did stop, sitting down on a little park bench beside the stage for a minute while she collected herself. Summer had no idea what was going to happen with Seth Cohen. And she truly had no idea if she wanted anything to happen at all. Their relationship had had so many ups and downs that it was hard to consider jumping in and starting the whole cycle again. Chances are it would end badly — it always did. But the beginnings were so good . . . well, they almost made up for all the heartache.

Almost.

Summer wished that the answer would magically appear to her, that she would look up and there would be some sign from above telling her exactly what she should do about Cohen. Then she could stop worrying and let fate run its course.

But when she looked up, she didn't see a sign — she saw the security guard from the front gate, and he was thundering straight toward her.

Summer let out a terrified little squeak and jumped up from the bench. She made a beeline to the door of stage twenty-four, hoping she could get to Grady before the guard got to her. At least the door was easy to spot — there was a big red light flashing above it.

Summer sprinted the last few steps. There was a girl with a walkie-talkie sitting on a folding chair outside the stage. She sprang to her feet when she saw Summer coming, but Summer figured she was probably another security person, and the best course of action would be to barrel past her. Summer made it to the door, grabbed the handle, and yanked.

She set one foot inside and stopped, surprised. Every single person in the place swiveled their heads toward the door and stared at her! Even Grady, who was lying on a couch in the middle of the set, smack-dab in the middle of a love scene with April, pulled his lips away from hers and looked at Summer.

"Cut! Cut!" A short, bearded man in a baseball cap leaped up from a chair and stalked toward the camera, a string of expletives exploding out of his mouth.

"Who the *!@^# opened the &@*(%-ing door in the middle of a %*$!#*-ing take?!"

Everyone was still looking at Summer. She gulped, then plastered on her best smile. "Hi. I was looking for Grady?"

Grady blinked, and the bearded man, whom Summer figured was probably the director, turned his wrath from the cameras to her. "Didn't you see the light flashing?" he screamed at her.

Uh-oh. "Yes," she admitted.

"Do you know what that light means?"

"Um —"

But the director didn't give her a chance to answer. "It means we're in the middle of a take! It means the cameras are rolling! It means you just cost us over twenty thousand dollars in ruined footage."

"I'm really sorry," Summer said. "But since you've stopped *anyway*, can I have a quick word with Grady?

Grady looked at her, confused. "Do we know each other?"

"I was at your birthday last year. Remember? At Luna Chicks?"

A vague memory flickered across Grady's face. "Whassup?" he said. It was unclear whether he remembered her or not, but Summer couldn't worry about that right now. Not with everyone still staring at her.

"Can I get a picture with you? Please? It's for charity."

"Oh!" said the director, in a bright, sarcastic voice. "Well, if it's for charity, then I guess it's *fine* that you're putting us behind on our shooting schedule. If it's for *charity*, I'll take the picture myself!"

"Actually?" Summer handed him the camera and scampered over to stand next to Grady. "That'd be great."

For a long minute, the director stared at the camera as if he wanted to hurl it at Summer's head, then he heaved a sigh, giving up. "If it'll get you out of here so we can get back to work," he said, and snapped the shot.

"Thank you, thank you, thank you," Summer said, taking the camera and the picture back from him. "Sorry again about messing up your scene."

She zipped back out the door and bumped right into the security guard, who was waiting outside.

"Let's go," he said brusquely, clamping a heavy hand on her shoulder and shoving her toward the exit.

"Um, sir?" Summer said, meekly letting herself be dragged away. "We need to stop and get my friend."

"Your friend needs to stop getting all up in my grille!" shouted the mud-splattered man onstage. Clad only in a thong and go-go boots, he clomped down the steps to where the audience was sitting, one dirty fist raised menacingly at a shrimpy guy

59

holding the microphone. Shrimpy's girlfriend had just implied that the people on the stage liked to roll around in more than just mud, and that was apparently the final straw.

The irate hoggie lunged into the audience, intent on doing some damage. Marissa, who was seated on the aisle two rows away from the stage, shrank back against the person sitting next to her, not wanting to be drawn in any way into the ensuing fracas, but fortunately, the host, Pat Diamond, stepped in before the hoggie could reach his target.

Unfortunately for Marissa, however, they stopped right in front of her chair, so she was treated to a closer view of the hoggie's pale hairy thighs and grimy thong underwear than she would have wished on her worst enemy. Under usual circumstances, such a sight would have made Marissa lose her lunch. But after the last hour of watching the otherwise-normal people onstage cavort and play in the mud like a group of lust-starved piglets, this final spectacle only made her want to laugh.

Frankly, the whole show made her want to laugh. Who were these people, Marissa wondered, and how did they ever manage to find one another? Marissa couldn't imagine going on TV and announcing some of the things she'd done to the world — not that she'd ever done anything like this!

And the audience was just as bad as the show's guests! Didn't any of these people have jobs? The middle-aged man in the chair next to her had told her before the show started that this was his thirteenth time as part of the studio audience. Thirteen times! It was crazy! What sort of person would voluntarily choose to spend their day watching this garbage?

Well . . . herself, for one. But she was being ironic when she watched it. Was it possible that all these other people were secretly laughing at the show, too? Maybe being in the audience at one of these shows was the newest incarnation of hipster camp, like watching *The Brady Bunch* or wearing leg warmers.

Marissa checked out the new guy at the microphone, searching for signs of amused detachment. Brown polyester shirt with a Texas sunrise embroidered across the chest (she knew it was a "Texas Sunrise" because those words were also embroidered, in bright orange thread, on the left breast pocket) and jeans with a crease running down the front of each leg. Both balding *and* acne-ridden — it made Marissa want to cry. Someone that hopeless couldn't possibly be enjoying the show for the mock value, could he?

The sad sack leaned into the microphone and addressed a girl onstage who was so covered with filth and dust that she looked like Ma Joad. "Yeah, this is for that girl there? That one on the, uh" — he glanced at his hands, making an "L" with his left thumb and index finger — "left?" Saliva pooled on his bottom lip as he spoke. "Yeah, you'd be hot if you cleaned yourself up a little, baby. So you take a shower and I'll take you out."

So much for assuming he was mocking the show — Marissa thought he was too tragic to even be mocked himself. But the rest of the audience was going crazy, clapping and hooting for the girl to respond. Pat Diamond hopped up onto the stage and tilted the microphone toward her.

"Gosh, that's a really enticing offer," she said, in a wry, cynical voice that made Marissa want to stand up and cheer, "but I'm afraid that me on a date would blow your mind."

The men in the audience booed, but Marissa laughed out loud. Finally, someone else with a sense of irony. Unable to resist her shot at trailer-park-style fame, Marissa rose to her feet. She grabbed the microphone Pat Diamond was passing around the crowd and shouted out the most sardonic phrase she knew: "You go, girl!"

The crowd went wild, and Marissa beamed, for an instant believing that the applause was for her. A second later, when she saw that the APPLAUD signs were lit and they had broken for a commercial, she felt like a fool.

But that didn't come close to the humiliation she felt a second later, when she saw Summer standing at the top of the stairs, her arm still captured by the security guard, motioning to her that it was time to go. God — she was still holding the microphone — she hoped Summer hadn't witnessed her moment in the spotlight.

She got up and followed Summer out to the gate. The guard shoved them out of the exit with a stern "And don't come back," and Summer and Marissa walked back to the street to wait for the bus.

"I can't believe you got us banned from the studio," Marissa said, but Summer just grinned.

"But I also got us this —" she said, holding up the Polaroid of her and Grady.

Marissa grinned back at her. "That's fantastic!"

"That's fantastic?" Summer mimicked. "Is that all you're going to say?"

"What else do you want me to say?" Marissa asked.

Summer gave her a knowing look. "You know. Come on, say it."

Marissa sighed, busted. "You go, girl!" she told Summer, and the two girls were still laughing when the bus pulled up a few minutes later.

9

"That's fantastic," Seth said, helping himself to another bite of Ryan's Cuban sandwich. "That's like the best thing I've ever eaten."

"Well, stop eating it," Ryan grouched, pulling his plate out of Seth's reach and shielding it with his arm. "You have your own lunch."

Seth poked at his burger dispiritedly. "But I like yours better."

"I told you to get a Cuban sandwich when we ordered," Ryan reminded him. "But you thought it sounded gross."

"Pork and pickles does sound gross," Seth said. "Who knew it would taste so good?"

Ryan gestured out the window of the diner at the 256 pigs they had just finished counting. "Seems to me, if you're eating at Farmer John's restaurant, it's a given."

Seth sighed and took a bite of his burger. "Well, my people don't believe in eating pork anyway," he consoled himself.

64

"Then why did you order bacon on your burger?" Ryan teased.

Seth responded by throwing a french fry at him, and Ryan laughed, grabbed the check, and stood up. "Ready to go? The girls'll probably be back at the hotel by now."

"Yes!" Seth brightened at the thought. "Let's go meet the girls." He got up from the table, too, snatching the last bit of Cuban sandwich and stuffing it in his mouth as he followed Ryan out the door.

They walked down the street to the bus stop, clocking the dozens of kids from the scavenger hunt who were clustered around the mural, busy getting the answer to clue number four.

"Guess we aren't as far ahead as we thought," Ryan said, peering down the street for any sign of the bus. He nudged Seth with his elbow. "Check the schedule and see when the next bus is coming, would you?"

"Look —" Seth said, pointing at a bus idling at the curb on the next block over.

"That's a tour bus," Ryan said, then stared in surprise as Seth took off toward it. "Seth! That's the wrong bus —"

"Come on!" Seth called over his shoulder, racing to catch the bus before it pulled away from the curb. He reached it just in time, jumping up onto the bottom step just as the door was about to close.

Ryan was right behind him but stayed on the

street, giving a tug at Seth's sleeve. "What are you doing? This is a bus for tourists."

"I know," Seth answered. "Look —"

He pointed at the big sign advertising all the stops the tour would take you to. On the list, right beneath the Farmer's Market and Griffith Observatory, were the words Angel's Flight. "Wasn't that the first clue?"

The tour bus driver was tired of waiting. "On or off?" he shouted at the boys.

"On!" Ryan said, jumping on the bus.

Seth grabbed a pamphlet from the tour guide describing all the sights, and the boys found a couple of empty seats.

"Nice work," Ryan said as they sat down.

"Guess I don't need glasses after all." Seth leafed through the pamphlet, searching for Angel's Flight. He found the listing and read the description. "Oh, snap!" he said.

"Snap?" Ryan gave Seth a look of disbelief. "What are you, Salt-n-Pepa?"

"Fine. Then I guess I won't tell you what the Angel's Flight is. You can just wait and see for yourself."

"Fine," Ryan answered.

"We'll see how fine you think it is when we get there," Seth said ominously, and directed his gaze to the Coca-Cola Bottling Plant the guide was describing out the right-hand window.

*   *   *

"Oh, snap," Ryan said, staring up in dismay at the Angel's Flight, a funicular railroad that carried people up the steep side of the mountain between Hill and Olive Streets. The tracks traced a nearly vertical line up the incline, so the train itself seemed to hang precariously in midair. "No way am I getting on that thing."

Seth came back from the booth where he was buying tickets and stood beside his friend, trying not to be amused by Ryan's terror . . . and not succeeding.

"The entire ride lasts less then a minute," Seth told him comfortingly, reading from the pamphlet. "It's the world's shortest railroad. Besides," he added, as Ryan started to turn green, "you can't have a funicular railroad without having fun!"

"Why don't you go ahead, and I'll wait down here for you," Ryan said.

"Come on," Seth cajoled, "I'm sure it's perfectly safe. Besides, I already bought you a ticket." He held the scrap of paper out to Ryan, who looked at it like it would bite.

"Yeah, I just don't see it happening," Ryan said, watching as the train inched its way back down to the ground. "So you go, enjoy the view, and I'll be here when you get back."

The train touched down and the doors opened. The first people off were the sixth graders they had met at the coffee shop that morning.

"That was AWESOME!" the red-haired kid shouted, racing past them.

The chatty little math-whiz kid was right behind him, jumping up and down in front of his mom, who looked considerably more harried than she had when they saw her in her car that morning. "Can we go again, Mom? Can we, can, we, can we?" the kid begged.

"Don't you want to keep solving the rest of the clues?" the mom asked wearily.

"Okay," he agreed, then chased after the red-head, shouting, "Wait up!"

Ryan and Seth watched them go, then Seth turned to Ryan, wiggling the ticket enticingly. "The Gummi Worms weren't afraid to ride on the widdle twain," he said.

Ryan rolled his eyes. His fear of heights was no secret to his friends, but that didn't mean he was willing to be shown up by a bunch of eleven-year-olds. "Gimme that!" he said, grabbing the ticket from Seth.

And the two boys boarded the train for a ride to where the angels take flight.

"Angels *nothing* — it was hell!" Ryan complained to Summer and Marissa. "They hoist you to the top of the mountain in this tiny little box, then plummet you down to the ground at, like, a hundred miles an hour."

"Six," Seth interjected. "Six miles an hour. Old ladies could make it up the path quicker than that train."

"There wasn't even a safety bar," Ryan added.

"You must be a lot of fun on a ski trip," Summer joked, but Marissa patted his arm sympathetically. "Well, you solved another clue and that's all that matters."

"At this point, getting something to eat is all that matters to me," Summer added.

By the time the boys had finished riding the funicular railroad and Ryan had breathed into a paper bag to quell his panic attack, it was late enough that the kids were starting to think about dinner. Seth insisted he had read about an amazing new restaurant in Silverlake that they all had to try, so Ryan called Marissa's cell phone and they met an hour later at the bus stop a few blocks away.

The only problem was that Seth couldn't remember the exact address of the restaurant, so the kids had been wandering up and down Hyperion Boulevard for the better part of an hour, looking for it.

"Seriously, man, let's forget the restaurant and grab a taco or something," Ryan said, but Seth shook his head.

"No, you guys, it'll be worth it, I promise. I just don't know why we can't find — aha!" Seth caught sight of the marquee across the street and gestured triumphantly. "Welcome to King Tut's."

The other three looked dubiously at the massive carved doorway, flanked by two huge inflatable palm trees.

"What is this place?" Summer asked, and Seth beamed.

"Best Egyptian cuisine in the city."

Ryan looked around desperately for a taco stand, but Seth gave him a little nudge. "Trust me — it'll be great."

The kids walked down a long rickety staircase to the dining room. It was smoky and full of dark, burly, mustachioed men. The walls were covered with red velvet, the lighting was all paper lanterns, and instead of chairs, everyone was sitting on big embroidered cushions. It looked like an opium den.

"Told you it'd be great," Seth said.

"Sure," Summer said, in a voice that was anything but. "Who needs fresh air and clean silverware anyway?"

As they waited for the host, who was seating the party ahead of them, Summer, worn out from all the walking, leaned up against a large wooden box with a Plexiglas top that was on the floor.

Marissa looked over at Summer and let out a little squeak of terror.

"Uh, Summer, you might not want to lean on that," she said in a strangled voice.

"Why not?" Summer asked, then looked down and shrieked herself. The wooden box she was leaning against was actually an open sarcophagus, with the Plexiglas protecting the mummy lying inside.

She leaped away from it, brushing frantically at the elbow that had touched it.

"Ew! That is the most disgusting thing I've ever seen!" she gasped.

"Are you kidding? That is an actual mummy found at a dig site in Khirbet Iskander. It's the *coolest* thing I've ever seen," Seth said, and Ryan nodded. He ran his fingers over the symbols carved on the lid and gave a little shiver.

"This is amazing," he said. "Just think, this person lived three thousand years ago. He might have helped build the pyramids. And look how well preserved he is. You know, they still use some of the same methods of preserving bodies that the Egyptians developed today."

Summer, however, failed to appreciate the archaeology lesson. "I can't believe they keep that in the same room where they serve food. That's got to be a health code violation or something."

"It isn't real, though, is it?" Marissa asked.

"The review that I read of this place said that it was authentic."

Marissa looked at it doubtfully. "If it's really real, shouldn't it be in a museum?"

Seth shrugged. "Maybe he was some low-level slave. Those mummies are a dime a dozen."

"Whatever he was, now he's nauseating," Summer said with a grimace.

"You better watch what you say around him," Ryan teased. "He'll come back and curse you."

"Seriously, Summer," Marissa said, looking at the translation of the inscription carved into the lid of the sarcophagus. "'As I ruled in this life, so shall I in the next.' Sounds like he's coming back. For you!"

The kids laughed, and the host, an immensely fat man with a bright red fez on his head, bustled over to them, all smiles.

"You read that aloud three times," he told Summer in a heavily accented voice, his eyes twinkling, "then turn around in a circle three times, then knock three times on the lid, and you'll wake him up."

"No way," Summer said.

Seth reached out and knocked twice on the lid, but before he could knock a third time, Summer grabbed his arm, shrieking and giggling at the same time.

"Maybe we'll let him stay asleep for now?" the host asked, and Summer nodded. "Good!" he said. "Now, my friends, the best table for you!"

He led them through the restaurant to a mosaic-covered table, next to a huge painting of Anubis, the jackal god.

The kids sat down, and the host bustled off to get them water. Seth shot a glance at Summer. "Zagat's loved it here," he whispered somewhat worriedly.

"If I could survive the bus, I'm sure I'll survive this place," Summer told him, and grinned.

Seth grinned back, his smile a sudden flash of brightness in the dim lighting.

The air was suddenly thick between them, and Ryan and Marissa glanced at each other, aware of the shift in mood. *Maybe Seth's plan is working after all*, Ryan thought. Because for all their bickering, there were definitely sparks flying between Seth and Summer. And if love was in the air anyway — he stole another look at Marissa — who knew what the weekend would bring?

But if Summer wasn't sure how she felt about Seth, Marissa *really* wasn't sure how she felt about Ryan.

Not wanting to get caught up in the moment, Marissa shifted in her seat, changing the subject. "Did you ever see the movie *The Mummy*?" she asked Ryan.

Ryan blinked, surprised that he was actually a little relieved that it looked like Marissa and he were going to keep things casual. It was easier that way, especially since they were going to be together nonstop for the next forty-eight hours. Besides, Ryan frankly was happy to just relax and have fun. "Yeah, and it *sucked*," he answered her.

"Are you kidding?" Marissa stared at him like he was crazy. "I loved it."

"I loved it, too," Summer said, coming to her friend's defense.

Seth looked at her, astonished by this admission of bad taste. "Oh, come on. Brendan Fraser? *Please.*"

"I think he's cute," Summer informed him. "He looks kind of like Zach."

"Ouch!" Ryan said, laughing, as Seth winced at the mention of Summer's former boyfriend.

So much for sexual tension, Seth thought ruefully. But before the conversation could deteriorate any further, the waitress, a beautiful exotic-looking woman in harem pants and a sequined bra, came over and asked for their drink order.

"What do they drink in Egypt? Ouzo?" Marissa asked.

"Hekt," the waitress replied. "An ancient beer."

"I'll stick to iced tea," said Summer.

"We'll take four," Ryan said, "and some menus?"

"Oh, no menus," she answered. "We cook good dinner for you. Very tasty. Very authentic."

"Perfect!" Seth told her.

Summer shrugged. "It's definitely an adventure."

The waitress brought the drinks and set them down. Ryan took a sip of his, then his gaze drifted back over to the sarcophagus.

"What do you think the first person who ever found a mummy thought?" he asked. "I mean, the first contemporary explorer, who goes on an archaeological dig, and all of a sudden he finds these unbelievable tombs."

"I used to wonder that about dinosaurs," Seth said. "Could you imagine, if you'd never heard of them, suddenly stumbling across this giant fanged skull? It's too crazy."

"You'd think they were dragons," Marissa said, then sat up straighter in her chair, giving a little wiggle of excitement. "You guys — the clue, 'Come face-to-face with a dragon'? Maybe they're talking about dinosaurs."

"You're right," Seth said, snapping his fingers. "I bet that's it."

Ryan pulled the list of clues out of his pocket and smoothed it down on the table. "Is there a museum in L.A. that has dinosaurs?" he asked. "Maybe the Natural History Museum?"

"No," Seth said. "We went there on a field trip in eighth grade. A mammoth disappointment."

"Hey," Summer said, the word *mammoth* striking a cord. "What about the La Brea Tar Pits?"

Seth shook his head. "Seventh-grade field trip. Another disappointment."

"The tar pits might not be the answer to that clue," Ryan said, looking at the list, "but check out number seven: 'Don't get stuck on La Brea.'"

"All right!" Marissa said as the kids clinked their glasses together happily. "We'll go there tomorrow. That's four clues finished. The Smears are cleaning up!"

The waitress came back to the table, carrying a huge platter covered with dishes.

"Thank god," Seth said. "I'm famished."

The smiley host hovered behind the waitress, helping ladle the food onto the kids' plates. It smelled good, but none of it was recognizable as anything the kids remembered eating before. The host set a heaping plate in front of Summer with a flourish, then waited with an expectant smile for her to try it.

Summer regarded her plate suspiciously, then tried a tentative forkful of something dark brown and crumbly. It was delicious, and she smiled at the host, already scooping up a second bite. "Ooh, that's so good. What is it?" she asked.

"*Mombar mahshy,*" he told her, "stuffed beef sausage."

The other kids also dug in, trying each dish as the host and waitress pointed it out.

"*Feteer bel asaa.*" The host piled a spoonful of

homemade cheese and spinach on Marissa's plate.

"Yum," Ryan mumbled, his mouth full. "What's this one called?"

"*Biram ruz* — goat in a pastry," the waitress explained.

Seth looked at his crowded plate. "What's this one?" he asked, pointing.

"That's plain steamed rice."

The kids stuffed themselves until there wasn't a scrap of food left on any of the plates, then leaned back in their chairs, perfectly content.

"So. What's the plan for tonight?" Summer asked.

"Go to the hotel and crash," Seth said sleepily.

"Cohen! We're in L.A. We can't just sleep."

"But we got up really early today," Seth whined.

"Too bad. We're in the city, and we're going to do something cool."

"Okay," Seth conceded. He pulled out the guidebook pamphlet he had picked up on the tour bus. "I'll find us something to do."

"Yeah, I said something *cool*?" Summer said, rolling her eyes at the tacky little pamphlet.

"Hey, there are lots of cool things in here," Seth said defensively. He started leafing through it. "There's . . . Knott's Berry Farm. Or Grauman's Chinese Theater. Or — here, we could get a star map and tour the stars' homes." He set the pamphlet down. "Okay, you're right, it's lame."

Ryan picked up the pamphlet himself, flipping through the pages.

"We could go to a club," Marissa suggested halfheartedly. "The Viper Room?"

None of the others looked wildly enthusiastic about this suggestion. "I'm pretty tired," Seth said. "I don't want to go somewhere where we'll have to stand around all night."

"How 'bout a movie?" Summer said.

"It seems a shame to come all the way to Los Angeles to do the exact same thing we could do at home," Marissa said.

"I've got it — let's go back to the hotel and crash," Seth repeated. The others ignored him.

"Why don't we . . . solve another clue?" Ryan said, grinning.

Seth shook his head. "My brain hurts. Four is enough for one day. Let's save the rest of them till tomorrow."

"Too late," Ryan said, "because I think I just solved one."

"Oh my god!" The other kids got a burst of energy and leaned in. "What is it?"

"Well, the clue was 'You might see Merlin there,' so I figured it's something about magic or King Arthur or something like that, right?" Ryan said excitedly.

"Or fishing," Summer chimed in.

The others looked at her blankly. Then —

"No, that's a *marlin*," Seth told her.

"Ah. Right." Summer considered being embarrassed, then decided not to. "So what'd you find?"

"Magic Castle," Ryan said. "It's a club for magicians in Hollywood. That's gotta be it, right?"

Seth nodded. "Merlin was a magician, he lived in a castle — good job, buddy." He held out a fist for Ryan to bump. Which Ryan did, somewhat self-consciously.

"We are on *fire*," Summer said happily. "We're going to win this thing, and Autumn Cabot will be so humiliated she'll want to die." Summer raised her glass to toast the others and looked startled when a geezer slumped in a corner lifted his own in return.

"So, Magic Castle's nearby, it's open until two — what do you say we go check it out?" Ryan suggested.

"Ugh. Can we do it tomorrow?" Marissa asked. "I couldn't eat another bite."

"Um . . ." Ryan looked at the others in confusion. "I don't think it's a restaurant."

"Anything with the word *castle* in it is a medieval-themed restaurant," Marissa said.

"She's got a point," Seth said.

"They'll call us wenches and make us eat turkey legs and the waiter will say things like 'methinks the damsel needs more grog.' I *hate* those places."

"I kind of like them," Summer said. "Last time I went to Medieval Times, they made me princess and I got to wear a tiara all during dinner."

79

"Was this for like your eighth birthday or some-thing?" Seth asked, finding it all pretty adorable.

"It was last winter," Summer admitted.

"Tell you what," Ryan promised Marissa, "we'll swing by there to snap a picture for the scavenger hunt, we won't eat a single bite, and if anyone calls you a wench? I'll punch him out."

Marissa gave him her best smile. "Then what are we waiting for?"

THE OC

11

"What do you mean, we can't come in?" Summer asked, outraged. The four kids were standing in the entryway to Magic Castle, being stonewalled by a bouncer, three hundred pounds of muscle in a tux, who looked neither magical nor medieval. Nor very sympathetic, for that matter.

"What part don't you understand, princess?" he answered. "No guest pass, no admittance."

"Okay," Ryan said. "How do we get a guest pass?"

"Do we need to ask the king?" Marissa chimed in, still convinced that the place was a theme restaurant and that the bouncer was just waiting for them to play by the rules.

But he just gave her a funny look and turned to let inside an elegantly dressed man and woman, who walked up to the door accompanied by a short, goofy guy in a velvet cape.

"Evening, Hal," the goofy guy said to the bouncer. Hal smiled back at him.

"You performing tonight, Joe?"

"I might have a trick or two up my sleeve," the goofy guy said, and the three people went inside.

"So what's the deal, you have to dress like Dracula to get in?" Summer said.

"'Dracula' is one of the best magicians in the country right now," Hal told them. "Furthermore, he is a member of this club. If you would like to come in, you need to find a member to accompany you or, barring that, give you a pass."

"Or," Seth said, a lightbulb going off, "if we were magicians ourselves, we could come in, right?" He gave Hal a disarming smile, then reached out and, only fumbling slightly, pulled a quarter from the gigantic bouncer's ear. "Huh? Huh?" he asked encouragingly, holding the quarter out for Hal to take.

The bouncer regarded him blank-faced and unblinking until Seth sighed and put the quarter back in his pocket. "I guess you don't want to see my knotted rope trick," he said sadly, and Hal shook his head.

"You kids need to get out of here so I can get back to work," he told them.

Ryan gave it one last try before admitting defeat. "Look, we're doing a scavenger hunt. Can't you just let us in for five minutes?"

"You scavenge yourself up a guest pass, and you can stay as long as you like," Hal answered, and turned away as more magicians walked up to the entrance.

*　　*　　*

Five minutes later, the kids were shuffling deject-edly along Sunset Boulevard.

"Maybe we solved the clue wrong," Ryan said. "But I was so positive that was it."

"There's got to be another way in," Marissa said. "Should we go back and see if there's a back door or an open window or something?"

"I don't want to mess with that stupid bouncer," Seth said. "Did you see how he dissed my coin-in-the-ear trick?"

"*Dissed*?" Ryan said. "What's with you and the eighties hip-hop slang today?"

"Nothing," Seth said, starting to smile, "just that that's a really hard trick, and that guy was whack."

"Was he way mad whackity-whack?" Ryan asked.

"You got served, Cohen," Summer said, shaking her head. "But I give you props for your magic skillz."

"Yeah, where'd you learn how to do that?" Marissa asked.

"I got a Li'l Svengali Box o' Tricks for my bar mitzvah," Seth said. "I can separate interlocking rings, make a handkerchief change colors, and pull Captain Oats out of a hat."

"Nice," Summer said, in a voice that was unclear to Seth whether she was being sarcastic or not. "Maybe you can put on a little show when we get back to the hotel."

That reminded Ryan — "You *did* reserve rooms for us at the hotel, right?"

"I booked our room last week," Seth said, then tried to look innocent as the other kids stopped.

"Room," Ryan asked, "or *rooms*, as in more than one?"

"Well . . ." Seth started, and then winced as Summer smacked him. "How many times do I have to tell you not to hit me before you'll stop?" he asked indignantly.

Summer responded by smacking him again. "You only booked one room for the four of us? What were you thinking?!"

"I was thinking that — uh, that we could send the money we saved to charity," Seth said, scrambling to come up with an answer. He caught Ryan out of the corner of his eye and gave him a conspiratorial wink.

Ryan sighed and shook his head. "Great *plan*," he said.

"Maybe the hotel will have another room available," Marissa told Summer, but Seth gasped.

"The money you would spend on that room is for *charity*," he scolded. "Think of the children who are suffering."

"You'll be the one suffering if we have to sleep in the same room," Summer threatened.

"Come on, it'll be fun," Seth said. "It'll be like old times."

"Yeah, because last time it turned out so well," Summer said.

"Wait, are you talking about San Diego? Or Tijuana?"

"I was actually thinking of you picking up that hooker in Vegas —" Summer said, but Marissa interrupted.

"Can we not talk about *any* of the old times?" she asked, and Ryan nodded.

"Fine," Seth said agreeably. "But remember this — I changed my bad bus karma, so here's our chance to eliminate our bad hotel voodoo too."

"Fine, whatever, let's just go," Summer said, picking up the pace, but Marissa held out a hand to stop her.

"Wait, guys. It's still early. Why don't we go in there first?" She gestured to the building across the street, a comedy club.

The others looked at it, not terribly inspired.

"The Laugh Factory? No thanks," Seth said.

"Seriously, Coop, have you lost your mind? It's a comedy club. They're so not funny."

"I know," Marissa said, "but look who's on the marquee."

"'The magical stylings of the Great Mysterioso,'" Seth read off the sign above the door of the comedy club.

"Maybe we can scavenge that guest pass after all," Marissa told the others.

"Beats sitting in a hotel room with Cohen," Summer teased, and this time, she was the one who got smacked, as the four kids crossed the street and went into the club.

THE OC

12

"Have you lost your mind? Are your eyes playing tricks on you? Or are you simply seduced by the marvelous magic of Mysterioso?"

The magician onstage, a pudgy young guy with a spangled wizard's hat perched awkwardly on his head, waved a wand over a bowl full of goldfish. "Now behold, a fish that flies!"

He tapped the wand on the rim of the bowl . . . and nothing happened.

Mysterioso made a comically puzzled face. He tapped the wand again. Still nothing. He held the wand to his ear, shook it, tried again. Nothing. Feigning frustration, he tilted his head back and held the wand up to his eye, like he was peering through a telescope, and a huge puff of bright blue smoke came out, hitting him in the face.

The audience chuckled. Mysterioso tapped the bowl again, and one of the fish rose out of the water and swayed in the air above the bowl. "A fish that flies! Great heavens above, what's next? A fish that disappears?!"

He flourished the wand — and a puff of red smoke shot out the back of it, making the audience laugh again.

Seth, sitting at a small table near the stage with the other three, nodded appreciatively at Mysterioso's shtick. Even Summer was laughing, but her smile changed to a look of disgust when, unable to make the fish disappear with his wand, Mysterioso made it disappear by popping it into his mouth and swallowing.

"Ew," Summer said, loud enough for Mysterioso to overhear.

"Ah, another young lady dazzled by the great Mysterioso's charms," he deadpanned. The audience laughed, and the magician walked to the edge of the stage near where the kids were sitting.

"I need an assistant for my final trick," he said. "Perhaps my lovely young critic would care to volunteer?"

"Not if I have to put anything in my mouth," Summer said, still grossed out by the goldfish.

The audience laughed and clapped, and Marissa nudged the horrified Summer. "Go on," she urged.

Summer got to her feet and climbed onto the stage. "You're not going to do anything like saw me in half, are you?" she asked dubiously.

"Nope," Mysterioso said, wheeling out a box with three guillotines suspended above it. "I'm going to chop you into quarters."

Summer was the opposite of happy about

climbing into the dirty, coffinlike box in her $800 dress, and she was more than a little worried about just how sharp the blades hanging over her really were, but she decided to be a good sport, if for no other reason than it might help them score a pass to Magic Castle and beat that little snot Autumn.

So she waved merrily to the crowd as she clambered into the magician's box, and she screamed good-naturedly and wiggled her toes as the guillotines dropped and she was chopped into four pieces.

After Mysterioso had "mistakenly" put her body back together again in the wrong order a few times, and she was puffed with purple and orange smoke, and she endured a couple of bad-taste jokes about the tribulations of dating a magician, Summer was released from the box safe and in one piece.

Her friends clapped louder than the rest of the crowd put together as she stepped off the stage and made her way back to the table. As Mysterioso was taking his bows, Seth gave Summer a provocative look.

"New fantasy number three," he said.

Ryan gave him a strange look. "Summer *butchered* is your new fantasy?"

"No, Summer the magician's assistant is," Seth answered. "I'm picturing doves, and a sequined costume like they wore in *Desperately Seeking Susan.*"

Summer shook her head. "I think you've got enough fantasies to go on now," she told him.

"Fantasies yes, drinks no," Seth said, and got up from the table to fetch another round.

"So?" Marissa asked. "How'd they separate you into pieces like that?"

"A magician never reveals her secrets," Summer said.

"Bravo," Mysterioso said, coming up to their table. "I knew I chose the right person to assist me in keeping the mystery intact."

He held out a hand and Summer shook it, introducing herself and the other kids.

"Come on," Marissa wheedled, "at least tell us where the goldfish went."

"You saw," Mysterioso said. "I ate it."

"Come on, you did not," Marissa said. "That's too gross."

"And mean to the poor little fish," Summer added.

"What can I say? A man's got to eat," the magician answered.

Seth returned from the bar and put the drinks down on the table. "Great show," he told Mysterioso.

"We were just talking about the goldfish," Summer told him.

"Carrots, right?" Seth said, and the girls squealed and clapped.

"Ha! I knew you didn't eat a real goldfish," Marissa said.

Mysterioso looked a little put out. "Could you tell from the audience that they weren't real?" he asked, but Seth shook his head.

"No, they looked great. I just figured you lifted it from the Amazing Cavalieri," he answered, referring to the name of the magical act performed by Joe Kavalier in Seth's favorite book, *The Amazing Adventures of Kavalier and Clay*.

Mysterioso's whole face brightened. "Oh my gosh," he said. "You're the first person I've ever met who got that reference."

"Are you kidding?" Seth answered, "'Please don't —'"

"'Please don't eat the pets!'" Mysterioso finished the name of the magic trick along with him, and the two guys laughed and clapped each other on the back like they were long-lost brothers or something.

"Huh?" Summer asked, but Ryan cut her off.

"Forget it," he told her. "Seth has interests we'll never begin to fathom."

As Seth and Mysterioso started gabbing about all things magic, Marissa leaned in to the conversation. "Have you ever heard of Magic Castle?" she asked the magician. "Because we'd really love to go there."

"How about tomorrow night?" Mysterioso answered. "You'll come as my guests. I insist."

The kids all thanked him, and as he and Seth made a plan for the next night, Marissa gave Ryan a wink. "Score!"

There were no additional rooms available at the hotel.

"Score!" Seth silently mouthed at Ryan as they trailed the girls to the elevator. Ryan drew in a breath, then let it out, exasperated. When was Seth going to realize that his schemes to get Summer never worked?

Then again, he realized, as Marissa fumbled to slide the plastic key card into the slot on the door, Seth and Summer did keep getting back together every time they broke up. So maybe, as pitiful and catastrophic as his machinations seemed, Seth was on to something.

But not this time, Ryan decided, as they opened the door to the tackiest hotel room he'd ever seen. This plan? Never going to work.

"Oh my god," Summer said, wrinkling her nose as she surveyed their home away from home for the next two nights, "it looks like a Cherokee threw up in here."

"That's gross," Marissa said. "True, but gross."

The room was an abomination of Santa Fe style. Indian-print blankets on the bed, dream catchers on the walls, shelves shaped like a cactus, everything painted sand and aqua.

"Are you kidding?" Seth said. He gestured at the giant portrait of a Hopi warrior skinning a buffalo, which was hanging on the wall above the beds, and grinned. "These are world-class accommodations."

"Third world, maybe," Summer said, gingerly moving aside the jackalope statue looming on the nightstand and setting her purse there instead. "Why didn't you book us a room at the Chateau Marmont or somewhere cool like that?"

"Because everyone from Harbor is staying at the Chateau," Seth replied. "Here we've got some privacy."

"Look, it's too late to do anything about it tonight," Ryan said. "Let's just go to bed and get some sleep."

"At least with the lights out, you won't be able to see the decor," Marissa said. She pulled a shirt out of her purse to sleep in, and Summer shrugged, digging in her purse for her own pajamas.

Ryan unzipped his backpack and took out a clean T-shirt and pair of boxers, then noticed Seth standing awkwardly by the door. "What?"

"You guys all brought a change of clothes?" Seth asked, inwardly kicking himself.

"We're not going back to Newport until

Sunday," Summer said. "You didn't bring anything with you?"

"I forgot," Seth mumbled. He turned to Ryan accusingly. "How come you didn't remind me?"

"Do I look like your mother?" Ryan said. "Besides, why do you think I've been carrying around this backpack all day?"

Seth shrugged. "Well, no problem, just lend me something, okay?"

"I only brought enough for me," Ryan said.

"Okay . . ." Seth did a quick sniff-check of the shirt he was wearing. "This'll probably last me until Sunday, as long as I don't run or do anything to work up a sweat. And I can sleep *al fresco,* so problem solved. Now, who's gonna let me use their toothbrush? Summer?"

"Ew! Cohen! No way!" Summer took a step back. "You can't wear the same clothes for three days, that's disgusting. And you are *not* going to sleep naked in the same room as me."

"I'll second that," Ryan said.

Seth held his hands out helplessly. "Well, what else can I do?"

"The gift shop in the lobby was still open," Marissa told him. "I bet they have some really nice things there."

"Yeah, I'll bet," Seth mumbled. He walked to the door and looked back at the others. "Ryan? Want to come with me?"

"Go," Marissa said casually. "It'll give us girls a

chance to get changed for bed." She glanced down at the baby-doll tee she had brought to sleep in. If she'd known she'd be sharing a room with Ryan, she'd have picked something a little less revealing. At least if he was gone, she wouldn't have to parade across the room from the bathroom in front of him in it. Even though Ryan had seen her wearing less than that a million times at the beach or back when they were dating, it still seemed a little too intimate for him to see her dressed for bed.

Despite her offhanded tone, Ryan could hear the edge in her voice, so he followed Seth out the door. "I'll keep him away from the moccasins and loincloths," he told the girls.

"Oh, ha-ha," Seth said, annoyed, and they headed back to the elevator.

"So? Whaddaya think?" Seth asked.

Ryan looked at the rack of T-shirts Seth was leafing through. The one in front said "FBI" in big white letters, with FEDERAL BOOB INSPECTOR printed in smaller letters underneath. "I think the girls won't let us back in the room if you show up with that."

"I'm not talking about the shirts, I'm talking about Summer. She seems like she's coming around, huh?" Seth held an orange MY AUNT WENT TO CALIFORNIA AND ALL I GOT WAS THIS LOUSY T-SHIRT shirt up to his chin and regarded himself in the gift shop mirror for a minute, then put it back on the rack and kept looking.

"Really? To you, that's 'coming around'?" Ryan asked.

"What? She's totally hot for me," Seth said.

"Yeah, making her question your personal hygiene was a really sweet move," Ryan answered. "I'm surprised she didn't fall all over you."

"You joke," Seth said, "but I'll be the one laughing when Summer and I are back together again." He spotted a green shirt with HOLLYWOOD printed across the chest in crooked letters that resembled the Hollywood sign, and showed it to Ryan. "This shirt's kind of cool, right?"

"Get it," Ryan agreed, then turned the conversation back to the girls. "I wish I could read the signals as well as you can."

"You and Marissa?" Seth asked, raising an eyebrow. He added a couple pairs of boxers printed with tiny palm trees to the shirt, toothbrush, and razor in his shopping basket.

"I don't know," Ryan said. "Sometimes I think she wants to get back together, but then she'll draw back and — I don't know what it means. It's like she's afraid to even think about the possibility." He looked away, distracted, and tossed a jumbo-sized pack of sweat socks into Seth's basket.

Seth took the socks out, placed them back on the shelf. "Maybe you should go for it."

Ryan shook his head and gave Seth a rueful grin. "*I'm* afraid to think about the possibility."

"Well, maybe you'll both be inspired when

you see me and Summer all snuggled up in bed together tonight," Seth said, and headed for the checkout.

"You're sleeping with Ryan," Summer told Seth, crossing her arms across her chest. "Boys in one bed, girls in the other."

Marissa was already under the covers in the bed near the window, so Ryan shrugged and pulled the covers back on the bed by the door. Seth shot Ryan a look of betrayal, then turned back to Summer.

"I don't want to sleep with another guy," Seth said, but Summer merely pursed her lips, unmoved.

"Guess you should have booked two rooms, then."

"Come on —" Seth looked around for help, but came up empty. "What's the big deal? We've slept together before."

"Yeah, when we were *dating*," Summer said. "But we're not dating now, and I don't want you to get any ideas about trying something."

Seth looked shocked. "I wouldn't try anything."

"I don't know," Summer said, looking him up and down. "If we're lying in a bed together, you might not be able to control yourself."

"First of all," Seth said, wounded, "the Cohens are nothing if not gentlemen. Secondly, we've slept in a bed together when we weren't dating, and I didn't try anything then."

"When were we in bed together?" Summer asked, skeptical.

"When we went to Tijuana," Seth said. "And there wasn't any problem then."

"Yeah, if you don't call Marissa getting helicoptered to the hospital a problem," Summer retorted.

Seth winced. "Right, I forgot about Marissa OD-ing," he admitted. "But that wasn't because we shared a bed."

Summer took a deep breath. "Cohen —" she began.

"Hey!" Marissa piped up from the bed, annoyed. "Enough already!"

The kids all stared at her for a second, then Seth let out a breath, his shoulders slumping. "I guess I'm sleeping with Ryan."

"Don't try anything," Ryan warned him, and Seth made a face.

"Thank you," Summer said. She waited until both boys were in bed, then walked over to the light switch. "Besides, if anyone should be worried, it should be me."

"What? Why?" Marissa asked, lifting her head to look at Summer.

"Hello, I'm not the one who likes to date girls," Summer told her.

That made Marissa sit the whole way up, an incredulous expression on her face. "*One* girl. Singular. Besides, Alex and I —"

She broke off when she saw Summer was

laughing. The boys were laughing, too, so Marissa rolled her eyes and slumped back down on the pillow. "Shut up and get in bed," she said.

"Good night," Summer said. And, still laughing, she shut off the light.

THE

14

"Good morning!" Marissa said, throwing back the curtains and letting light flood the room. The other kids reacted like a pack of vampires, groaning and throwing hands in front of eyes to block out the sun.

"It's too early," grumbled Summer, who was sprawled across the bed, her face mashed straight down into the pillow.

"It's after eight," Marissa said, "and can you even breathe like that?"

"It's Saturday," Seth mumbled, his eyes still shut. "Go back to sleep."

Marissa walked over to the boys' bed and took a picture of Ryan and Seth with her cell phone's camera.

Ryan cracked open an eye to give her a baleful stare, then looked down at Seth . . . who was nestled up against him, his head resting on Ryan's chest.

Startled, he shoved Seth away from him. "Get off me!"

99

"Quit jostling me. . . ." Seth whined, then opened his eyes, too. When he saw where he was lying, he gave a little shriek and, instantly fully awake, sprang away from Ryan.

"Why are you making so much noise?" Summer said sleepily, barely managing to lift her head an inch off the pillow.

"It's nothing," Seth said, and Marissa laughed.

"I'll show you the picture when you get up," Marissa told Summer.

"No, you will not," Seth said. He struggled to his feet, wiping a trace of drool off his cheek with the back of his hand.

Ryan glanced down at his T-shirt, checking for wet spots. "If you drooled on me, I'll kill you," he said.

"You already practically killed me with your snoring," Seth answered.

"No, that was Marissa," Summer said, throwing up her hands to shield herself from the pillow Marissa threw at her.

"Shut up, I do not snore," Marissa said.

"But you do get up at the crack of dawn," Ryan said.

"It's quarter after eight," Marissa repeated, "and we've got five more clues to solve."

"Fine," Summer said, and sat up, throwing her arms out in a yawn. She blinked a couple times, then her eyes focused on Seth. Summer started laughing. "Oh my god, Cohen, what is up with your hair?"

Seth checked himself out in the bureau mirror. He had terrible bed-head, with his hair sticking straight up from his head like he'd been electrocuted.

"You look like Screech," Marissa said, and she and Ryan both burst out laughing.

"Please allow me my dignity," Seth said, waving a grouchy hand at them. He stumbled toward the bathroom. "I'm going to take a shower."

"Ooh, wait, I need to get in there first," Summer said, jumping out of bed.

But Seth shut the bathroom door in her face.

"Cohen!" Summer pounded on the door with her fist.

"Occupado!" Seth shouted through the closed door, then he was the one laughing, until the noise of the shower drowned him out.

An hour later, the four kids were all showered and dressed, and were helping themselves to the free continental breakfast buffet in the lobby.

"So what's the game plan?" Marissa asked. They had the list of clues and the maps spread out over the table, studying them as they ate.

"Why don't we hit the tar pits first, just so we can knock that off the list, then regroup and try to figure out the rest," Ryan suggested.

"Regroup? Are we splitting up?" Seth asked. "Because I could go with Summer."

"I meant reassess," Ryan explained.

"Of course you did." Seth nodded and took a

bite of doughnut. A dollop of bright red jelly squeezed out the end of the pastry and landed on the map. Seth scooped it up with his index finger, leaving behind a crimson smudge. "Sorry."

"Wouldn't it be weird if that stain marked the exact location of one of the clues?" Summer said.

"Spooky," Marissa agreed. She bent over the map. The jelly had landed on the publisher's name at the bottom of the map. "Does Rand McNally seem like the answer to any of the clues?" she joked.

"It's no worse than anything else we've thought up," Ryan said. He folded up the map and took a last slurp of coffee. "So — on to the tar pits?"

"Let's go!" Summer said, and they gathered up their things and set off on the second day of the hunt.

They walked down the street to the deserted bus stop and waited. There was a concrete bench to sit on, but it had some murky liquid dripping off the side of it, puddling on the ground next to it, so by unspoken agreement they all chose to stand.

The bus took so long to come, though, that they almost reconsidered sitting. "Where is it?" Summer demanded, shifting her weight from side to side. "We've been waiting forever."

Ryan double-checked the schedule. "It should have been here by now."

"If it doesn't come, does that mean we can take a cab without breaking the rules?" Summer asked, hope in her voice.

"I'm sure it'll be here any minute." Marissa took a step out onto the street to see if she could see it coming. She couldn't. "Well, let's just wait a little while longer."

"*Let's call the mayor, let's complain. Looks like the city's done it to us again,*" Seth started singing.

"What are you singing?" Summer asked, momentarily distracted from her boredom.

"Violent Femmes. 'Waiting for the Bus.'"

"That's not a real song, is it?" Marissa asked.

"Not a real song? It's an *excellent* song," Seth said. "'*Hey, Mister Driver Man, don't be so slow. . . .*'" He trailed off and grinned at his friends.

"Quite possibly the best song about buses ever written," Ryan added.

"No way," Marissa said, her eyes flashing a challenge. "Destiny's Child. 'Get on the Bus.' Now *that's* a good bus song."

"Nope, I got it," Seth said, snapping his fingers. "'Spadina Bus,' by the Shuffle Demons."

"Yeah, whatever, if you're going to pick some band no one's ever heard of," Summer told him.

"Are you kidding? Everybody knows the Shuffle Demons," Seth protested.

"Well, *I've* never heard of them," Summer said.

"Me neither," said Marissa.

"Me neither," Ryan added, smiling.

"Fine, if you want some boring populist AM radio garbage," Seth said, "how's this: *Kathy, I said as we boarded the Greyhound in Pittsburgh . . .*"

He stopped singing as the bus finally pulled up to the stop and they filed on.

The kids were happily surprised to find the bus nearly empty. They sprawled across the bench seats in the back, picking up their conversation exactly where they'd left off.

"I happen to like Simon and Garfunkel," Summer informed Seth, "but if you want the all-time greatest song about buses ever? 'Cars, Trucks, Buses,' by Phish."

The others regarded her with surprise. "*You* like Phish?" Ryan asked. "In a million years I would never have pegged you as someone who listens to Phish."

"There's nothing wrong with Phish," Summer answered defensively.

"Of course there isn't, sweetheart," Seth said, patting her arm like she was a very small child. "But I just thought up the all-time winner —" He looked around to make sure he had their full attention. "The Replacements. 'Kiss Me on the Bus.'"

The other kids all nodded. "Yeah, that's a really good song," Marissa said.

"Definitely," Ryan agreed.

"*If you knew how I felt now, you wouldn't act so adult now,*" Summer sang, and Ryan, Seth, and Marissa all joined in on the chorus.

"*Kiss me on the bus, kiss me on the bus.*"

As they sang, Seth gave Ryan a look: *See? Summer's coming around.*

And looking at Summer, smiling as she tried to

harmonize and got the whole group off-key, Ryan couldn't help but agree.

Phish wasn't the only surprise Summer had that morning. As the bus sped along Hollywood Boulevard and crossed Highland Avenue, she leaned over and hit the signal for the driver to stop.

"Um, I know you don't have a lot of experience on buses," Seth said, "but that's not like a stewardess call button on an airplane. The bus driver's not gonna bring you snacks and a pillow."

"How about a complimentary headset?" Summer asked sarcastically, standing up as the bus pulled to a stop at La Brea Avenue. "Come on, you guys, let's go."

"But — just 'cause we're on La Brea, it's still a really long way to the tar pits," Ryan told her.

"I know," Summer called over her shoulder, skipping down the step to the sidewalk. "Now come on!"

The other three looked at one another — with Summer already off the bus, they guessed they had no choice but to follow.

"Did you have so much fun waiting hours for the last bus that you wanted to enjoy the experience all over again?" Marissa asked, looking longingly at the taillights of the bus disappearing down the street.

"No, silly, I solved another clue." Summer held her hand out for the list, which Ryan dug out of his pocket and gave to her. "'Number nine: Share

105

some space with these leading ladies,'" she read. "'Dolores Del Rio, Anna May Wong, Mae West, and Dorothy Dandridge.'"

"Right," Seth said, not sure what Summer was getting at. "And you think these long-dead starlets are going to be hanging out at" — he glanced around at the buildings nearby — "Quiznos, enjoying a turkey sub?"

"No, I don't think that," Summer retorted, narrowing her eyes and flinging her arm out dramatically to point at a building down the block. "But I do think the best place to see a bunch of dead movie stars is . . . the Hollywood Wax Museum."

"The wax museum!" Seth smote his forehead with an open palm. "Of course! You are a genius!"

"Thank you," Summer said, traipsing toward the museum. "Please remember that the next time you start to act all Cohen-y."

"Cohen-y?" Seth asked. "What does that even mean?"

"You know," Summer said, searching for the right word. "Snide. Sarcastic."

"Mocking," Ryan chipped in.

"Trenchant, derisory, sardonic," Marissa added. The others looked at her, and she shrugged. "Princeton Review."

"I'm not snide," Seth protested. "Or any of those other things you said."

"Of course not," Ryan said. "And I'm sure none of the dead starlets at Quiznos think you are, either."

Seth stared at them for a minute, then turned and started walking toward the wax museum. "Gang up on me," he mumbled under his breath. "That's real nice."

"Aw, are your feelings hurt?" Summer asked. "Poor Cohen, so easily bruised, inside and out."

"You're like a marshmallow Peep," Ryan said, then clutched his arm as Seth slugged him. "Ow!"

"Yeah, I'd like to see a Peep merk on you like that," Seth told him, then pushed open the doors to the museum and went inside.

THE OC

15

"Well, that was a bust," Seth said, carefully picking the tomatoes off his turkey sub. "I sure am glad we took this little two-hour detour. Who cares that we didn't solve the clue — it was worth it to see that rockin' statue of Mr. Miyagi."

"Um, *snide*," Summer responded, doctoring her sandwich with a spoonful of hot peppers.

The kids had combed the museum for statues of the four starlets and come up short. Mae West was in long-term storage, they didn't have statues of Dorothy Dandridge or Dolores Del Rio, and neither of the security guards they asked had ever even heard of Anna May Wong. Frustrated and hungry, they'd finally left the museum and crossed the street to grab some lunch at Quiznos.

"It was a really good idea, Sum," Marissa said.

"Not good enough," she replied glumly. "I just can't imagine where else we could 'share space' with those actresses."

"Were they ever in a movie together?" Ryan

asked. "Maybe we're supposed to rent a DVD of them or something."

"I don't think so," Marissa said. She ripped open a bag of potato chips and started crunching them.

Summer reached over and helped herself. "This isn't as fun as it was yesterday."

"Look, we're still probably way ahead of all the other teams," Seth said. "We'll go to the tar pits now, Magic Castle tonight — we've already got a ton of clues solved."

"Try *five*," Summer said grouchily, and Seth looked to Marissa and Ryan for confirmation.

"Now who's the snide one?" he asked them.

"Summer has a point," Marissa said. "We've only figured out half."

"It's still early," Seth said, trying to rally them. "We can still win this thing. Don't give up now." He leaned close to Summer. "Would Phish give up? I think not."

"We should change our team name to the Terminators, because we *just won't stop*," Ryan said, allowing himself to be rallied. "We're determined, we're unflagging, we're" — he gave Marissa a poke — "help me out, SAT."

"Obdurate!" Marissa said. She wadded up the remains of their lunch and tossed them into the red plastic trash can. "Come on, guys, let's get back on that bus and win this thing!"

Summer looked at her friends like they were

crazy but got to her feet. "Go, team!" she said in the peppiest voice she could muster.

The four kids walked back to the place where they had gotten off the bus that morning. There was a small silver gazebo on the corner, with benches where they could wait. But as they walked up to the gazebo, who should they see walking out of it but Liesl and her team from Harbor.

"Omigod, you guys, are you having so much fun?" Liesl asked, bouncing up and down on her toes in front of them.

"Sure. How about yourself?" Marissa asked, as if it wasn't obvious.

Liesl gave them an entirely unironic double-thumbs-up. "Last night Ginny brought a tube of cookie dough back to the hotel room, and she ate so much, she yuked! It was totally gross. We made her sleep in the bathtub."

"That's too bad," Marissa said. She gave Ginny, who was sitting on the steps of the gazebo rummaging through a Gwen Stefani Le Sport Sac, a little wave. "Hope you're feeling better," she called.

Ginny gave her a single-thumb-up in response.

"How are you doing with the scavenger hunt?" Seth asked, moving as far away from Ginny as he could without being obvious.

"Sharing space with the leading ladies makes four down, six to go," Liesl said. "Baby-claps!"

Seth and Ryan exchanged a glance, but before they could ask her more about it, another member of Liesl's team shouted for her and Ginny to hurry up.

Liesl made a sad-clown face. "Guess I better motor. Bye-ee."

She hurried down the steps, but Summer was hot on her heels. "Liesl. Wait."

Liesl stopped, and Summer gave her a disarming smile. "You wouldn't want to give us a hint about that leading ladies clue, would you?"

Liesl looked at her, confused, then burst into laughter. "You're so funny," she said. "You almost got me. Okay, bye-ee."

Liesl skipped away after her team, and Summer made a face at her back. Why in the world did Liesl think she was joking? But when Summer turned back to the gazebo, she got her answer.

Seth was leaning against one of the silver pillars holding up the roof of the gazebo. The pillars were shaped like women, and at the bottom of the one Seth was leaning on was a little brass label that read: DOROTHY DANDRIDGE. Each of the four pillars was a statue of one of the actresses they were looking for.

Summer showed her discovery to the other three, and they made short work of taking a picture of each of them standing by a different statue.

With the pictures in their pockets and their spirits considerably lifted, the four friends sprawled on the gazebo steps while they waited for the bus. But who did they see coming toward them instead but the kids from Del Vista.

There were no parking spaces on the crowded street, so Chaz haphazardly swung his car to a stop in front of the steps the Harbor kids were sitting on, managing to block both a fire hydrant and a wheelchair ramp. The doors swung open before the car had come to a complete stop, and Mickey, Autumn, and the other cheerleader tumbled out.

"Hello, losers," Autumn said.

"Do you smell something?" Summer asked her, wrinkling her nose as Chaz shut off the car and came stumping up behind Autumn. "Oh, it's just your boyfriend. Never mind."

Chaz lifted his arm and gave his pit a sniff. Autumn elbowed him sharply in the side and Chaz dropped his arm. "Shaddup," he told Summer.

Autumn turned to her cheerleader friend and waved a manicured hand dismissively at the Harbor kids. "Isn't it sweet how they keep trying to solve the clues, even though they don't have a chance in hell of winning this thing?"

"For your information," Summer said, "we're practically finished."

Autumn narrowed her eyes. "How many clues have you solved?"

"How many clues have you solved?" Summer shot back at her.

Autumn hesitated for a split second, then her lips curled into a smug smile. "Eight," she told them. "And the wax museum makes number nine."

The Harbor kids exchanged a worried glance. If they really had eight . . .

"You're such a liar," Summer said. "No way do you have that many clues solved."

"Besides, you're totally cheating anyway," Seth added. "If you took the bus like you're supposed to —"

"The bus is for suckers," Mickey said.

"Well, you suck," Summer said, "so you should feel right at home on it."

"Well, you suck harder," Mickey responded, "so it's a good thing you're getting so much practice, because you're gonna need it tomorrow when we kick your ass at the finish line."

"That doesn't even make any sense," Seth said. "Practice doing what? Sucking?" He spoke to Mickey in a slow, careful voice. "You have to put the words together in your head first before you let them come out of your mouth. Now, think — what were you trying to say?"

Mickey stared at Seth, confusion clouding his features as he tried to remember. He finally gave up and settled on "Del Vista rules!"

Seth laughed and Autumn turned to her friends, furious. "Come on, guys, let's go take a picture of clue number nine."

The four Del Vista kids started away, and Chaz yelled back over his shoulder, "Have fun on the bus!"

The kids from Harbor looked at one another, their earlier good mood evaporated. "You don't think they actually have eight clues solved, do you?" Marissa asked.

"No way," Summer said. "She was just trying to psych us out."

"In any event, they're not going to find number nine in there," Ryan said, watching as the Del Vista team disappeared into the wax museum.

"But when they come back out, they'll figure it out, same as we did," Summer said.

"I wouldn't be too sure about that," Seth said. "That Mickey guy is as dumb as a box of monkeys."

"Still," Summer insisted mournfully, "they'll eventually figure it out, and then they'll just drive to the finish line in their nice, clean, air-conditioned car while we're still sweating on the bus."

"Not necessarily," Ryan said, bounding down the steps toward the street.

Curious, the other kids followed him to see what he had in mind.

Ryan walked up to a police car that was idling by the curb, the officers inside keeping an eye on the throngs of tourists wandering up and down Hollywood Boulevard.

The policeman in the passenger seat rolled down his window as Ryan approached. "Can I help you?" he asked in a gruff voice.

"Sorry to bother you, sir," Ryan answered respectfully. He pointed at the Del Vista kids' Mercedes. "But I was just wondering — is that car allowed to be parked there? It's blocking the handi-capped ramp."

"It's in front of a fire hydrant too," Marissa

added from where she was standing with Seth and Summer, admiring how clever Ryan was.

The policeman lifted his radio and pushed the TALK button. "Can I get a tow at the corner of Hollywood and La Brea?" he asked the dispatcher, then turned to Ryan. "We'll have it towed away shortly."

"Thanks!" Ryan said.

The four kids watched happily as the other officer walked over to the Mercedes and started writing parking tickets for it.

The tow truck arrived at the same time as the city bus did, and the kids climbed on it, watching out the window as the Del Vista kids' day was ruined.

"Seth?" Ryan asked as the bus turned the corner to head south on La Brea, and they settled back in their seats. "There's one thing I don't understand."

"Yeah?" Seth asked, and Ryan grinned.

"Who keeps monkeys in a box?"

THE OC

16

"How do you know if an elephant's been in your refrigerator?" Seth asked.

"Seth! Quit monkeying around and take the picture," Ryan ordered.

"No, seriously, guys, how can you tell?" Seth repeated, thoroughly enjoying making the others suffer.

The kids were standing outside the La Brea Tar Pits, by the sculpture of the mammoth family sinking into the tar. Still buoyed by their coup against Del Vista, they decided to have some fun with the picture and get creative. While Seth held the camera, Marissa hugged the baby mammoth, Ryan draped an arm around the father mammoth's trunk, and Summer, feeling especially adventurous, had scrambled up onto the back of the father like she was riding an elephant at the circus.

But the kids got more than they bargained for — the ground around the sculpture was slick with sticky tar bubbling up, and the air around the pits was stiflingly hot and smelled a bit like the wrong end of a mammoth itself.

Much amused by his friends' discomfort, Seth was dawdling as long as possible before snapping the shot.

"Seth! Come on!" Summer pleaded, but Seth shook his head.

"Not until you answer my riddle," he insisted.

"Footprints in the butter!" the other three all shouted in unison.

"Footprints in the butter," Seth cackled, taking the picture. "Funny when we were six, still funny at sixteen."

"That's the last time you get to take the picture," Ryan said, making a swipe at the camera.

"Besides," Marissa informed him, "those aren't elephants, they're mammoths."

Summer slid down off the back of the sculpture and started walking toward the rest of them. "That was so not funny —" she started to say, but then her foot hit a patch of tar and she slipped, landing flat on her butt in the grass.

"No, but *that* was," Seth said, holding out a hand to help her up.

Summer struggled to her feet and brushed the dirt and grass off her pants. But there was a big black splotch of tar on the back. "Oh my god," she said, like it was the absolute last straw. "My pants? Are ruined."

Marissa took a Kleenex out of her purse and dabbed at the stain. "I'm sure the dry cleaner can get this out. . . ." she said uncertainly. The Kleenex shredded in her hand, little bits of it sticking to the tar.

"Here, let me try," Seth said, but Summer stopped him.

"Touch my butt and die," she warned.

Seth shot her a wounded look. "I was only trying to help."

"Help by getting me a new pair of pants."

Ryan looked down, embarrassed about checking out Summer's butt. "It's not that bad," he said. "You hardly notice it."

"Not that bad?!" Summer was incredulous. "I look like Br'er Rabbit! I'm going back to the hotel to change."

Ryan glanced at his watch. "Uh, it's already after two, and we need to be at Magic Castle at seven. I don't think we have time to go back to the hotel if we're going to get through any of these other clues."

"I don't care! I am not walking around Los Angeles with asphalt on my ass," Summer said in no uncertain terms.

"Look, why don't we split up?" Marissa said. "Summer can go get changed, and we'll just call her when we figure out where we need to go for the next clue."

"I'm not taking the bus alone," Summer said, aghast at the thought, and Seth raised his hand.

"I'll go with you!" he said eagerly, then tried to downplay his enthusiasm. "I mean, since it's kind of

118

my fault you got tar on you in the first place. Since I took so long to take the picture."

"Fine, whatever, can we just go?" Summer said.

"Of course." Seth grabbed Summer's arm and started leading her to the street, before Ryan or Marissa could protest. "Good luck with the next clue!" And they were gone.

Ryan and Marissa looked at each other. "I guess it's just you and me," Marissa said.

"Guess so."

The only available place to sit was on a bench next to an ancient man so covered with wrinkles you could barely see his eyes. He was halfheartedly tossing pieces of bread to the pigeons pecking around his feet. The kids walked over to the bench, and he smiled and shifted to the end, so there'd be room for both of them to sit.

Ryan pulled out the list of clues, which was starting to become so creased and rumpled that it was a miracle they could still read it.

"Okay, let's see . . . you want to tackle that dragon one again?"

Marissa considered — then shook her head. "What else have you got?"

"Okay, here's one: 'Darling, it's better down where it's wetter.' Huh." Ryan thought about it. "What does that even mean?"

"Darling, it's better down where it's wetter, under the sea," Marissa sang. "That's a song from *The Little Mermaid.*"

"How in the world do they expect us to know that?"

"You're probably the only person doing this scavenger hunt who hasn't seen *The Little Mermaid*," Marissa said, teasing. "I guess you thought it wasn't masculine enough for you."

"Yeah, I was too busy shaving to watch it," Ryan said, facetiously flexing a bicep. "I couldn't be bothered with some silly cartoon."

"Says the boy who played Snoopy in his sixth-grade school play."

"Hey, Snoopy's tough," Ryan protested. "He hangs with his boy Woodstock, he bosses Charlie Brown around from on top of that doghouse. Don't underestimate him."

"Yes, he's a very manly beagle," Marissa conceded. "Now, can we get back to this clue?"

"Absolutely. What's under the sea?"

"Fish, sand —"

"Submarines." Ryan snapped his fingers. "I bet it's the submarine ride at Disneyland."

But Marissa shook her head. "Closed for renovation. Kaitlin went to a birthday party there a couple weeks ago and was upset that she didn't get to go on it."

"Hmm." Ryan thought for a minute. "Are there other submarines in Los Angeles?"

"There's the *Starlight* submarine in Catalina," Marissa said. "It's really cool. Only" — her face fell — "the tickets to it are something like thirty bucks a person. They probably wouldn't make the teams pay a hundred twenty dollars to solve a single clue."

"Yeah, that kind of defeats the purpose of doing this for charity," Ryan said. "Besides, Catalina's pretty far away."

Marissa caught a strand of hair in her fingers and twisted it as she thought. "Does Universal Studios have a *Hunt for Red October* ride?"

"Checky check!" the ancient man sitting on the bench next to them suddenly piped up. Ryan and Marissa turned to him, surprised — they had forgotten he was even there!

"Excuse me?" Marissa said.

"Checky check," the old man repeated. "There is a Russian submarine docked in Long Beach."

"Is that right?" The man looked so decrepit that Ryan wasn't sure how intact his mind was, and Long Beach was a long way to go if the oldster was actually remembering touring a sub at the 1934 World's Fair or something.

"The *Scorpion*. It's a Foxtrot-class diesel-electric attack sub from 1972."

Marissa shared a skeptical glance with Ryan. "And you say it's in Long Beach?" she asked.

"It's docked next to the *Queen Mary*," the old man said. He caught the look Marissa flashed at Ryan and sat up straighter. "I'm not senile," he groused, "I'm trying to help you."

"Of course, we're sorry," Marissa said, all apologies. "Thanks so much for the help."

"Yeah," Ryan added. "Sorry."

"Stupid kids," the man said, and got up from the bench and shuffled away from them. "Feh."

"Sorry," Marissa called after him, then turned to Ryan. "Oops."

Ryan raised an eyebrow. "What do you think? Put our trust in Wrinkles McGee, or —"

"— or give up?" Marissa finished his thought. "I guess we're going to Long Beach."

"I refuse to spend an extra hour and a half on the bus," Summer said, snapping her cell phone shut. "Those guys can handle taking a picture of the sub by themselves, because no way am I going to Long Beach."

"It's silly for all of us to go anyway, when we still have more clues to solve," Seth said.

They were still on the bus, basically parked in the middle of traffic. They'd left the tar pits almost half an hour ago but had barely made it a mile. Seth had considered suggesting that they just get out and walk because it would be quicker and smell better than where they were now, but he knew without asking that for Summer, almost any hell was better than traipsing around West Hollywood with a decomposed mastodon on her butt.

"You're right, Cohen," Summer said, pushing a damp lock of hair out of her eyes. "Let's figure out some of the other clues."

"Okay," Seth said.

They looked at each other silently for a minute,

then Seth said, "So . . . what are the other clues, then?"

"*I* know?" Summer replied. "Didn't you see them this morning?"

"Sure, but I didn't memorize them," Seth said.

"Me neither."

They sat in silence for another minute, then — "We could call Marissa back and ask her what they are," Seth suggested. But Summer shook her head.

"Coop said her battery was dying. We probably shouldn't use it up, in case they have an emergency or something."

"Right." Seth thought for a minute. "There was that one about the dragon."

"'Come face-to-face with a dragon.'" Summer brightened. "Let's solve that one."

"Okay."

Easier said than done. Another minute passed, then Seth let out a huge breath. "Maybe this'll be easier after you change your clothes. We won't be so distracted."

"Yeah, about that . . ." Summer turned in her seat so she was facing Seth square on. "I don't really have anything to change into. I mean, I was going to wear my jeans tomorrow, and I can't put the dress I had on yesterday back on. So I was think-ing, maybe we could go shopping really quickly."

"I happen to know that the hotel lobby gift shop has a fine selection of quality garments," Seth told her. He grabbed the hem of his T-shirt and pulled it taut, so Summer could get a good look at it. "Matter of fact, I bought this stylish shirt there on your suggestion."

"Cohen!" Summer protested. "You can't seriously expect me to wear something like that."

"You no likee?" Seth asked pitifully. "I try so hard to look nice for you, and this is the reaction I get?"

Summer cracked up, and Seth smiled. "Where were you thinking instead?"

"Fred Segal is just a couple blocks from here," Summer said.

"Well, it's no Ramada Inn News and Sundries," Seth said, "but I suppose it'll have to do."

"Did I get all the tags?" Summer asked, twirling around so the salesgirl could check out her cool new black pants.

The salesgirl nodded. "We've never had anyone wear the clothes out of the store before," she said snidely, and handed Summer back her credit card.

"I'll take the receipt, you can keep the attitude," Summer said. She grabbed the bag with her ruined old pants in it and headed out of the junior's apparel section to look for Seth.

She found him in the hat department with a brown leather fedora with a two-foot-long neon-red ostrich plume tucked in its brim perched awkwardly on his head.

"Who do I look like?" he asked her. He took a couple little tripping steps forward and back, swinging his arm around as though he were bran-dishing a sword.

Summer studied him. "Huggy Bear?" she guessed.

Seth stopped, disappointed. "I was going for Errol Flynn."

"That would have been my second guess," Summer said kindly.

Seth took the hat off and put it back on the rack. He picked up a British newsboy cap instead and tried that one on. "Crikey, I'm knackered!" he said in something approximating a Cockney accent. "The lift was broken so I had to take the apples and pears. I need a pint."

"*Now* are you doing Huggy Bear?" Summer teased. She put a huge fancy garden-party hat on her head and struck a pose. "How do I look? Ridiculous?"

"No. You look . . . beautiful," Seth said.

Summer's expression softened. "Cohen. What are you doing?"

"Nothing," Seth said. "You asked, so I told you. I think you look perfect." He waited a beat, then added, "Except for those crazy pants. Stop kidding around and put the real ones on."

"Shut up!" Summer said, laughing. "I love these pants. Seriously, don't you like them?" She did the same twirl she'd done for the salesgirl, but got a better reaction this time.

"Best. Pants. Ever," Seth proclaimed. "You want to go buy some shoes to go along with them?"

"No," Summer said. "The shoe department here is a zoo. I'm too tired to face it."

"Yeah, I'm pretty worn out too," Seth said. "I'm really draggin'."

As soon as the words were out of his mouth, Summer and Seth both froze, the idea hitting them both simultaneously.

"Do they have dragons at the zoo?" Summer asked, mentally crossing her fingers.

"They have Komodo dragons, I believe," Seth answered, "which we could easily come face-to-face with, if we went there."

"Oh my god!" They solved another clue! Summer squealed and threw her arms around Seth's neck. She and Seth jumped up and down, hugging. "We did it," she said happily, smiling up at him.

"We sure did," Seth answered, and before he knew what he was doing, he tilted his face down to hers and kissed her.

They leaned into each other, his mouth sealing her mouth, the sudden rush of blood to Seth's head making him feel like he was probably going to have a stroke and die right there in the hat department, but he actually wouldn't mind so much; it would be worth it to leave this earth feeling Summer's gorgeous soft lips against his own.

He wanted the moment never to end, so of course the next instant Summer was pushing him away, putting her hands on her hips to show the anger that she just couldn't get her face to register.

"Cohen! I can't believe you kissed me," she said, doing her best to disguise the jelly-kneed quaver in her voice.

"I know!" Seth said, wide-eyed. "How did that happen? And more important, how can we make sure it happens again?"

Summer let out a little bark of laughter. "It can't. We can't just kiss."

"Why not?" Seth asked.

Summer stared at him, completely at a loss for an answer. "Because . . . we have to go catch the bus."

Seth tried to conceal his smile. He hadn't planned this, but it was better than anything he ever could have planned. *"Kiss me on the bus,"* he sang softly, and now Summer's exasperation was real.

"Cohen!"

"Fine," Seth told her. "Just let me go pay for this hat, and we can get out of here."

"Don't you dare!" Summer ordered, laughing, happy for the chance to pretend things were normal between her and Cohen.

Because honestly? She had never felt more off-kilter in her life.

THE OC

18

"This is not normal," Ryan said, looking around the completely deserted pier. "In fact, it's downright —"

"Freaky," Marissa said.

Ryan looked at her out of the corner of his eye. "Come on, did Caleb Nichol spend six hundred dollars on SAT prep for 'freaky'? At least give me 'disquieting' or 'eldritch.'"

Marissa smiled and stepped a little closer to him. "I'm too pusillanimous to think up a big word."

The scene in front of them really was freaky. One minute they had been strolling along the busy boardwalk by the *Queen Mary*, where hundreds of tourists streamed in and out of the restaurants, shops, and attractions that lined the sidewalk. It was noisy and lively and bright. But the second they turned the corner to the pier where the Russian sub *Scorpion* was docked, it was like they had stepped into a ghost town.

The pier was completely abandoned — the

shops' windows were all boarded up, there was a chain-link fence with an enormous padlock barring access to the *Scorpion*, and there was no sign of life. The buildings cast giant shadows across their path, no noise from the main drag managed to filter through to this pier, there weren't even any insects buzzing in the air. It was desolate and lonely and really pretty creepy.

Ryan and Marissa stood in front of the locked gate trying not to freak out themselves.

"Where is everybody?" Ryan wondered. "This is like an episode of *The Twilight Zone* or something."

"Or that movie where the people got on the plane, and when it landed, they were the only people left on Earth," Marissa said.

"I thought that was *The Twilight Zone*," Ryan murmured. He reached out a hand and tested the lock on the gate — it held fast.

"Maybe this pier's been condemned or something, and we just didn't see the signs," Marissa said. She looked back over her shoulder toward the main drag — there weren't even any people walking past.

"Yeah, it's probably set to blow any minute now," Ryan said distractedly. "Or maybe there's just a poison gas leak or something." He tilted his head up to check the top of the fence — it really wasn't that high, and there was no barbed or razor wire protecting the top of it. So maybe...

"What should we do?" Marissa wondered.

"Maybe there *is* a *Red October* ride at Universal Studios. Or, what was that other movie? *U-521* or something? Bon Jovi was in —" She broke off, looking in puzzlement at Ryan. "What are you doing?"

Ryan had his fingers interlocked and was offering her a foothold. "Up and over," he said.

"You're kidding, right?"

Wrong. "Ryan," Marissa said, her eyes huge, "we can't break in to a Russian submarine!"

"Why not? We're not going to hurt it."

"What if we get caught?"

Ryan looked around — there was no one there to catch them. He held his laced hands out to Marissa again, and she impulsively stepped up onto them. Ryan boosted her to the top of the fence, then climbed up himself as Marissa scrambled over the top and let herself down on the other side.

"I can't believe we're doing this!" Marissa exclaimed.

Ryan put a finger to his lips, just in case there was a guard or someone, and led her down the narrow walkway to the *Scorpion*.

They got to the sub, which was half-submerged in the water, without seeing anyone else, and relaxed. Marissa jumped up onto the deck and held her arms up showcase-style to the call letters painted on the side of the ship, while Ryan took the picture. She started to jump back down to the dock, but Ryan stopped her.

"Don't you want to look around while we're here?"

Marissa hesitated, clearly tempted, and Ryan grinned. "Come on."

They went down the narrow metal steps into the submarine and began exploring. It was dim inside, with the only light coming from the sun filtering grayly through the portholes. There were valves and pipes everywhere, and the whole atmosphere was so dismal and claustrophobic that Ryan couldn't imagine spending an hour inside the sub, let alone months at sea.

"Cool, check this out," Marissa said, investigating a small room off the main passageway, and Ryan walked over to see what she was looking at. There were stained yellow spaceman suits hanging on a hook on the wall, and Marissa read the plaque next to them out loud for Ryan. "These are escape suits. It says here that if a sailor needed to get off the ship, he'd put this on and they'd fire him out of the torpedo tubes."

"No way," Ryan said. "How scary is that?" He walked over to a torpedo tube and stuck his head inside, peering up the dank passageway. "Think I'd rather drown," he said.

There was no answer from Marissa, and when he turned to look for her, she was gone. "Marissa?" he called softly. "Where are you?"

"*Ping!*" came her voice from outside the chamber.

Huh? "Marissa?" he called again, walking out into the main hallway.

"Ping!" was the same response, accompanied by giggling, coming from around the corner.

Ryan walked down the passage and found Marissa standing by the captain's quarters, laughing.

"What are you doing?" Ryan asked.

"I pinged you. Isn't that how subs communicate?"

Ryan also started to laugh, suddenly aware of their proximity, the small quarters forcing them to stand so close they were almost touching. The privacy, the shared joke, the captain's bunk, lonely and inviting.

Marissa also picked up on this intimate feeling, and they both stopped laughing as their desire started to grow. "Ryan," Marissa said softly, "we —" But she was spared from having to finish that thought by a sudden noise.

Heavy footsteps echoed down the passageway, and a police radio crackled. Ryan and Marissa looked at each other wide-eyed, romance instantly replaced by panic.

"Security guard!" Ryan whispered. Taking her hand, he tiptoed down the passage toward the exit, peeking around corners as he came to them to make sure they weren't about to bump into the guard.

Marissa followed, her heart beating so loudly she was sure it would give them away.

Finally they reached the exit hatch. Ryan and Marissa sped up the stairs and then raced for the gate.

Marissa didn't need a boost this time; she grabbed a handful of fence and hauled herself up, her shoes scrabbling for purchase in the narrow links. Ryan made it over the fence first, landing heavily on the ground. Marissa pulled herself over the top — and slipped.

Ryan caught her as she fell, and for a second they stayed in each other's arms, adrenaline coursing through them, their faces a scant millimeter apart. If Marissa thought her heart was thumping before, it now beat so furiously she was sure it would burst. Ryan's eyes locked onto hers, he dipped his head, but an instant before his lips brushed hers, the security guard came huffing up out of the sub and ran toward them.

"Hey, you kids!" he shouted, chasing after them, and Ryan and Marissa broke apart, sprinting down the pier away from the guard . . . and away from having to consider what that kiss would have meant, at least for a little while.

"Guess who kissed!" Seth whispered to Ryan, following the girls into Magic Castle. Mysterioso had met the four kids at the front door a few minutes earlier. He ushered them past a different but equally humongous bouncer, then led them down the impressive Corridor of Stars, a long hallway plastered with posters and playbills of magic acts from all over the world.

Mysterioso stopped to show Marissa and Summer a few of the highlights, and Seth seized the opportunity to discuss the afternoon's events with Ryan. The two boys hadn't had a second to be alone together since Ryan and Marissa got back from Long Beach, and Seth was close to bursting with his news.

"It was fantastic," Seth told Ryan in a low voice, glancing over at Summer to make sure she wasn't in earshot. "I macked on her in the middle of her favorite department store. We're totally getting back together."

"Is that what she said?" Ryan asked.

Seth looked down at the ground uncomfort-ably. "No. She told me to stop kissing her. But it doesn't matter, because the plan is totally working."

Ryan gave Seth a sideways glance. "You're not the only one it's working for," he told his friend. "Me and Marissa? Came really close."

Seth's eyes widened. "To having sex?"

"No," Ryan said, irked. "To kissing."

"Wow!" Seth said. "So maybe we need a sig-nal, for tonight, if one of us is knockin' boots —"

"Don't say 'knockin' boots.'"

"If one of us is making progress, so the other one doesn't interrupt." He thought for a second. "We'll hang a sock on the door."

"Seth," Ryan said practically, "we only have one room. A sock on the door's not going to help."

"You're right. Huh." Seth looked at Ryan. "Whaddaya know, there's a flaw in the plan."

"Guess who kissed?" Summer said to Marissa, examining her makeup in the ladies' room mirror, then digging in her purse for her lip gloss.

Mysterioso had to go prepare for his evening's performance back at the comedy club, so he left the kids in the Grand Salon bar. And while Ryan and Seth waited for a table, Marissa and Summer ducked into the ladies' room to freshen their makeup and indulge in a little girl talk.

"You and Seth?" Marissa asked, surprised. "No!"

"Yes!"

"You slut!" Marissa said, delighted. She set her comb down on the counter and twisted the cap off her own lip gloss. "So? Are you guys back together again?"

"No," Summer said, then thought about it for a second. "No," she repeated, deciding for real, "it was just a lark. What happens in L.A. stays in L.A. and all that." She picked up Marissa's comb and ran it through her own hair.

Marissa leaned close to the mirror to add a second coat of mascara, eyeing Summer's reflection out of the corner of her eye. "Summer?"

"Yeah?"

"I came really close to kissing Ryan today, too," she admitted.

"Oh my god," Summer breathed. "Does this mean you like him again?"

"I don't know," Marissa said. She gave her reflection a final check, then smiled ruefully at Summer. "I don't know what I was thinking, it just happened."

The girls walked back to the bar, Marissa lost in thought. She didn't know what she had been thinking earlier, but she sure as hell knew what she was feeling. There were sparks between her and Ryan, which she hadn't felt in a long time.

But along with the tingling thrill she got whenever she was close to Ryan came the memories of how disastrous they had been together. She'd sworn the last time she and Ryan broke up that she would be sensible from then on and not get romantically entangled with him again. But it was hard to be sensible when he was so close to her she could see the flecks of gray in his blue eyes, feel the heat rising from his skin.

Just the thought of what almost happened — and what could still happen that evening — made Marissa so nervous that when she got to the table, she gulped down the soda Ryan had ordered for her in a single swallow and grabbed a passing waiter to order another, thinking that she wouldn't mind something stronger.

Summer glanced from Marissa to Ryan and, even though no one was talking, decided to change the subject. "Where should we take the picture for the scavenger hunt?" she asked brightly. "I vote we do it in the Parlor of Prestidigitation."

"Let's go," Seth said, getting up from the table. The others followed.

The Magic Castle was made up of a series of rooms, all featuring different sorts of magical acts and performances. There was a dining room, two bars, several theater-type stages, and a couple of smaller theme rooms. There was a show taking place in the Parlor of Prestidigitation, so they couldn't get in there to take their picture, but they stood in the back of the room and watched the act.

A hypnotist was onstage, enchanting various members of the audience. As they watched, he made a middle-aged businessman leap around the stage like a chimpanzee, and convinced a tall blond woman that the number seven didn't exist, which caused great amusement when he had her count the fingers on her hand and came up with eleven.

When the show ended, the kids clapped enthusiastically, then let the crowd carry them along into a small, ornately decorated room, with a mahogany grand piano in the center of it. There was no one seated at the piano, but the keys were moving as it played "Don't Cry for Me, Argentina."

"It's bewitched," explained the waitress who came over to take their drink order. "Ask it to play any song in the world, and it will."

Marissa cast a guilty look at Ryan before ordering a soda with vodka, but he was busy examining the piano with the others.

"Any song?" Seth asked, and the waitress nodded.

"'Tiptoe Through the Tulips,'" Summer said, and miraculously, the piano started to play.

"Give it another one," Seth said, amazed.

"Okay," Ryan said, "how about 'La Marseillaise.'"

"What's that?" Summer asked.

"The French national anthem."

The piano began to play it. "Cool!" Summer said. "Okay, here's a hard one: 'Wake Me Up Before You Go-Go.'" The piano started playing the Wham song, and the kids grinned at one another. "I think this is where we should take the photo," Summer said, and the others nodded.

The waitress came back with Marissa's drink, and Summer asked her to take their picture. The four kids clustered around the piano, but as the waitress snapped the shot and handed the camera back to them, they heard a saccharine voice say, "I'm surprised the lens didn't break."

Summer looked over and, to her dismay, saw Autumn Cabot at the bar, paying for four bottles of beer. "What are you doing here?" she asked, and Autumn rolled her eyes.

"Duh," she said, and, carefully balancing the bottles, carried them away to her team.

Summer turned back to her friends. "God. There's no escaping that girl. She's like a human virus."

"Well, let's not let her spoil our night," Seth said. He put a comforting arm around Summer's shoulders, but she squirmed out from under it.

"She won't," Summer said, not wanting Cohen to think that because they'd shared one kiss he could touch her anytime he liked.

"Where's the waitress?" Marissa asked, looking around.

Ryan glanced at her empty glass suspiciously. Any inclinations he had about getting back together with Marissa were supplanted by the fact that she always had to get drunk, no matter what the occasion. He was a fool for even thinking things could work out between them. "Don't you think you should slow down? Too much soda's bad for you." he told her.

Marissa flinched. Who did Ryan think he was anyway, telling her what to do? Sure, they had some chemistry that afternoon, but she was only drinking to relax, it wasn't like she was getting drunk or anything.

"I can have three sodas if I want," she said, a hard edge to her voice.

"This'll be four," Ryan muttered , adding under his breath, "And just *what* are you drinking?"

Summer and Seth traded a look. "I'm going to go check out the rest of this place," Seth told Ryan and Marissa.

Summer was already on her feet. "I'll go with you."

They walked out of the room and down the long hallway which led to the other stages. They stopped to watch a magician making a rabbit disappear over and over, its fur turning a different color each time it reappeared.

"God, what is it with those two?" Summer said, referring to Ryan and Marissa. "They can't go twenty minutes without fighting."

"Thank god we're not like that," Seth said. He came up to stand close behind Summer and put his hands on her shoulders, impulsively massaging them.

But for the second time that night, Summer squirmed away from his hands.

"What?" Seth asked, anger hiding the hurt in his voice.

"Stop touching me," Summer said. "Just because we kissed doesn't mean I'm going to do anything with you."

"I didn't want to do anything anyway," Seth said, storming off.

He walked down the hall to the Palace of Mystery and walked up to the bar. He slumped down on a bar stool. Only then did he notice who was sitting beside him: It was Autumn's cheerleader friend, the fourth member of the team from Del Vista.

"Great," he said with a sigh. "Just my luck." He held his hands up in surrender. "Go ahead, let me have it."

"What?" the cheerleader said, looking puzzled.

"Say whatever mean, nasty thing you need to say, then go away and leave me alone."

The girl's expression grew even more confused. "Why would I say something mean to you? I don't even know you."

Now it was Seth's turn to look puzzled. "You're Autumn's friend from Del Vista, right?"

"Yeah, and you're that boy from Harbor who keeps getting Mickey to make an ass of himself," the girl said and hid her mouth behind a hand as she giggled.

Seth raised an eyebrow, disarmed by the way this girl was acting. "I'm Seth," he said.

"I'm Felice."

"Felice?"

She nodded apprehensively.

"Hi."

Felice braced for the inevitable, but it didn't

come. "Thank you for not singing 'Feliz Navidad' at me," she said, beaming at him.

"Well, I'd have to be a jerk to do that," Seth said.

"Chaz and Mickey have made that stupid piano sing it six times already."

Seth studied Felice as if she were a puzzle he was trying to piece together. "Can I ask you a question?"

"It's an old family name," she preempted.

"Different question. You seem really nice and cool —"

"Thanks." Felice blushed prettily, and Seth felt a tug in the pit of his stomach.

"So, why are you hanging out with those horrible horrible people?"

"They're my team," Felice said simply.

"Yeah, but — why are you even on a team with them?" Seth asked.

"Autumn and I are cheerleaders together, so when she asked me, I said okay." Felice leaned in, touched his arm. "She's not as awful as she seems. I guess she just hates that Summer girl. She said that when they were eight, they went to camp together and Summer tried to set her on fire."

Seth laughed, and then Felice began laughing, too, and that was how Summer found them, a moment later.

"Cohen!" she said, shocked and outraged. "What do you think you're doing?"

Summer couldn't believe her eyes. She'd gone looking for Cohen to apologize to him. She'd been harsher than she intended in brushing him off, and the only reason she'd acted so mean was because she really wasn't sure what she wanted from the relationship, and she didn't want to lead him on and end up hurting him.

Summer had no idea how she was going to put those feelings into words, but she figured when she saw him, she'd just say whatever came naturally. Imagine her surprise to find him consorting with the enemy! Apparently Summer had been misreading Seth's signals, if he could forget about her so quickly and be hitting on another girl — the best friend of her biggest rival! — in the mere minutes since they had their fight.

Seth looked up at her guiltily. "This is Felice —" he said feebly.

"I know who she is. She's a spy for Del Vista."

"That's crazy," Felice said, but Summer ignored her.

"You think she's flirting with you because she likes you? She's only trying to get you to give away the answers to the rest of the clues, so their team can win the hunt."

"She's not —" Seth started, but Summer was on a roll.

"She's going to go running back to Autumn with whatever secrets you tell her. And she'll drop you faster than I did," Summer said, then turned on her heel and stalked out of the bar.

Seth watched her go, a sinking feeling in his chest. Felice moved her hand from his arm to his knee. "That's not true, what she said," she told him.

"I know," Seth said. "Sorry about that."

Felice shrugged. "It's not your fault. So, you want to have a drink?"

Seth gave her a troubled smile. "I think I better go find Summer," he said, and walked out of the bar, Felice watching him as he walked away.

Summer was nowhere to be found, and neither were Ryan and Marissa. The four kids had scattered to separate ends of the Magic Castle, so when they finally came together again, as the club was closing and all the lights were turned on bright, they had all had time to endlessly rehearse their own side of the argument. They were all tired, and in some cases a little drunk, and none of them was feeling particularly happy with anyone else.

They walked out the front door of the castle, and Seth stood back to let Summer go down the steps in front of him. As she brushed past him, instead of saying thanks, Summer snarled, "Waiting for your girlfriend?"

"Oh, grow up," Seth snotted right back at her.

"Both of you grow up," Marissa said. She had a pounding headache and couldn't bear to listen to another second of them squabbling. "You drive me crazy with your endless fighting."

"Us?" Seth said, outraged. "You two are the ones always fighting."

"Leave me out of it," Ryan snapped.

The kids continued their bickering all the way down the long driveway to the street. They walked to the bus stop and Seth pulled the bus schedule out of his pocket.

He looked at it, then at his watch, and shook his head. "Goddamn it."

"What?" Ryan asked sharply.

"We've missed the last bus."

The kids looked at one another in furious disbelief. "How are we supposed to get back to the hotel?" Summer whined. "There are no cabs anywhere!"

"How do you think?" Seth said bitterly.

And without another word to one another, they turned and began the long, hostile, silent walk back to the hotel.

THE

20

Less than six hours later, and feeling no less hostile, the four kids sat glowering at one another by the hotel's breakfast buffet, sullenly nursing cups of coffee and refusing to be the one to apologize first.

Summer finished her coffee and reached for the pot to pour a second cup. There was only enough coffee left for one person, so Seth tossed back the rest of the coffee he'd been drinking in a single swallow. His arm shot out and grabbed the pot before Summer could get hold of it, and he dumped all the remaining coffee into his own cup.

Summer gave him a disgusted look, but Seth just smiled in return. "Mmmmm," he said, circling the cup beneath his nose to savor the aroma. "Nothing tastes as good as that second cup." He took a big swallow — and spit it out, fanning at his freshly burned tongue. "Gah!" he cried. "Hot! Hot!"

Summer laughed meanly, and even Ryan and Marissa smirked — served Seth right for acting like a jerk.

"Well, this has been *such* a nice weekend,"

Marissa said in a fake cheerful voice. "I'm *so* glad I got to spend so much time with you all."

"You were the one who suggested a stupid scavenger hunt in the first place," Summer muttered.

Marissa started to protest, then stopped herself. It wasn't like Summer hadn't come up with any better ideas at the time. She decided that she wasn't ready to give up being angry just yet — not until Summer admitted her own complicity on it all.

"Let's just finish the clues and get this over with," Ryan said, and Seth nodded.

"Lezz goah thuh soo," he said, holding an ice cube against his singed tongue.

The other kids gave him a look: *huh?* so he dropped the ice cube back in his water glass. "Let's go to the zoo," he repeated, and the kids pulled themselves wearily to their feet.

As resentful as the kids all still felt, it was pretty hard to stay angry while spending the morning at the zoo.

They arrived early enough that it wasn't crowded yet, and the sunlight dappling through the leafy trails was still cool and pleasant.

They picked up a map of the zoo at the entrance and set off to locate the Komodo dragon. As they strolled down the path that would take them to the animal habitats, they passed a coffee stand.

Seth stopped, digging in his pocket for some money. "Anybody want coffee?" he asked in a reconciliatory tone. "Summer? Second cup tastes the best."

"I'll take a cup," Ryan said.

"Me too," said the girls, and a minute later, they were all happily caffeinating as they wandered toward the lizard house.

"The Komodo dragon's enclosure should be down this way," Ryan said, starting down the paved trail. The girls followed him, but Seth didn't move.

"Look at this," Seth said, staring up at a huge bamboo sign that stretched across the pathway to their right. "Red Ape Rain Forest. When did they build this?"

Marissa shrugged. "Hasn't it always been here?"

"No," Seth said definitively. "The last time I was here, they had a monkey house and that was it."

"When was that?" Ryan asked.

"Third-grade field trip," he answered.

"This weekend has really been a trip down memory lane for you, hasn't it?" Summer said, but Marissa cocked her head to one side, thinking.

"I remember that field trip," she said. "In Mrs. Nagorsky's class. I was afraid to go into the monkey house because I was wearing my new yellow windbreaker, and Scott Ellison told me the monkeys would think I was a banana and eat me."

Ryan and Summer started laughing, but Seth was nodding. "Right. You were the banana. And I was wearing my Batman costume because I wanted to see the bats, but we ran out of time before we got to their cage."

149

"Oh my god, you used to dress up as Bat Boy. I forgot all about that," Summer said. "That was so cute."

"Can we maybe go see the bats now, since we didn't get to back then?" Seth asked.

"We can go see the *Komodo dragon*," Ryan said, not unkindly.

"Fine," Seth said sulkily. "Just 'cause you were still living in Chino back then and never got to go to the zoo, you don't have to take it out on me now."

"I got to go to the zoo," Ryan protested. "In kindergarten." He smiled at the memory. "The teacher kept referring to the lions and tigers as 'big cats,' and telling us how dangerous they were and how they were man-eaters. I was afraid of any cat bigger than a kitten for *years*."

"God, I was the only normal one of all of us," Summer said.

"*Was* being the operative word, of course," Seth said, and Summer stuck her tongue out at him.

Feeling better about themselves and one another, the kids made it to the Komodo dragon's cage and snapped a picture of it.

"All right! Is that all the clues?" Seth asked, but Ryan shook his head.

"Two left." He smoothed out the hopelessly rumpled clue sheet. "'Go Dutch' and 'Seal the deal with a group shot.'"

"Seals!" Marissa and Summer said in unison.

"*Yeah*, they are," Ryan agreed, and they turned back up the path to the pen where the seals lived.

*   *   *

"Where are they?" Summer asked, leaning over the railing precariously far and staring down into the pit where the seals weren't. The sign above the pen said SEAL VILLAGE, but the habitat itself was completely empty. No water, no rocks, and certainly no seals.

A zookeeper in a blue polo shirt and work boots sauntered past, and Marissa stopped him. "Do you know where the seals went?"

"Their habitat's being remodeled," the zookeeper told them, "so until it's finished, all the residents are visiting their cousins at the Long Beach Aquarium."

He strode off, and Ryan kicked one of the sign pillars with his sneaker. "Long Beach! We should have gone there yesterday when we were at the *Scorpion.*"

"Well, let's solve the last clue first, and then we can hit the aquarium before we go to the finish line," Summer said.

"Good idea. And you know where there are benches where we can sit down?" Seth said. "The *bat house.*"

The other three sighed. Seth wasn't going to be deterred.

A few minutes later, they were sitting on the molded plastic benches inside the bat house, a darkened room with a mesh net bisecting it. Over the kids' heads, separated by the netting, hundreds of bats swooped and flew. Summer flinched every time their wings would brush the net, and she was gripping the edge of the seat so hard, her finger-tips were white.

"'Go Dutch,'" Ryan reminded them of the final clue they had to solve. "What do you guys think?"

Seth's eyes widened. "Oh my god," he said, lowering his voice to a whisper, "they want us to buy pot!"

"No," Ryan said, flatly.

"Think about it," Seth insisted. "Why else does anyone go to Amsterdam?"

"There are a couple good museums there," Marissa said. "The Rijks Museum has some great Vermeers."

"Oh, right, like anyone cares about art when there's all that pot around," Seth said.

"Think about it, Seth," Ryan said patiently. "Why would the A Dream to Share Foundation, a charity that helps sick kids, ask us to go buy drugs?"

"Maybe . . . some of the kids have glaucoma?" Seth said.

"Please be serious so we can get out of here," Summer begged.

"What else, *besides pot,* do you find in Holland?" Ryan asked.

"Um, tulips, wooden shoes, Edam cheese," Marissa suggested.

"Windmills," Seth added, and Summer stood up.

152

"Great! Now let's get out of here."

The other kids didn't budge. "We have to solve the clue first," Marissa reminded her.

"There's a windmill in Pacific Palisades," Summer said. "Now come on, let's go, before those bats get out!"

"My stepmonster came here to detox," Summer said, when Marissa asked her how she knew about this place. The four kids were walking across the wide green lawns of the Personal Enlightenment Center, headed back to the bus stop.

The Personal Enlightenment Center was a New Age rehabilitation center and sanctuary, incorporating therapeutic elements from a variety of cultures in its beautiful grounds. There was a Buddhist temple, a duck pond, a Native American sweat lodge, and, sure enough, a windmill. On a different day, it would have been nice to spend some time wandering around the center, but now that they had all the clues solved, all four kids were eager to finish up the hunt and make it to the finish line. So as soon as they snapped the photograph, they started hurrying back to the street.

"Detox?" Marissa repeated, surprised. "Was your stepmom an addict?"

"No," Summer said, her feelings for her dad's

154

wife transparent, "she was taking Vicodin for her nose job when whosie from *Friends* had that pain-killer addiction, and she wanted to play it safe."

The other kids were saved from having to respond to that by a shout that made them stop in their tracks. Liesl and her team were running across the grass toward them, all yelping like hyenas.

Marissa tried really hard not to roll her eyes, as Liesl skidded to a stop in front of her.

"Are you stalking us?" Liesl asked, then dissolved in giggles.

"How's it going there, Leez?" Marissa asked.

"I can't believe you guys thought of this place, too," Liesl said. "Great minds . . . where?!" She laughed at her own joke, since no one else was.

"Have you guys figured out all the clues?" Summer asked her.

"All but one," Liesl said, "but the final clue is about to learn that there's a new sheriff in town."

"A sheriff named the Harbor School Hyenas?" Seth couldn't resist asking.

"Don't be mean," Summer scolded under her breath, but Liesl didn't seem put off by the comment at all.

"Darn tootin'," she said. "See you at the finish line!" Then she set off after her team, her "Yip! Yip! Yip!" shattering the tranquil atmosphere.

The four friends made it to the bus stop without running into anyone else they knew. Even the view from the front gate was calming — the Pacific Ocean crashing onto the shore. People walked along the beach, and a series of gray rocks jutted out of the water along the waterline.

Only . . . those gray rocks were moving! Those weren't rocks at all, Seth realized — they were seals!

Excited, he ran across to the beach, calling to the others to follow. "You guys," he said, realizing, "if we don't have to go to Long Beach Aquarium, we can go straight to the finish line. We have an actual shot at winning!"

Excited, the kids got as close to the seals as they dared, and Marissa held the camera out to an uptight-looking man in an ironed jogging suit who happened to be walking past.

"Would you mind taking a picture of us?" she asked him.

"Sure," the man said. He took the camera from her and inspected it. "What kind of film are you using?"

"Uh — it's a Polaroid," Ryan told him.

"They make slow-speed Polaroid film for shooting out of doors and in bright settings," the man said. "You get a much better picture."

"Good to know for next time," Ryan said. "But it'd be great if for now you could just shoot us with what's in there."

"I guess," the man warned, "but the quality's going to be poor."

"All that matters to us is that we're all in it," Summer told him.

"And a seal!" Seth added. "You've got to make sure a seal is showing, too."

The man peered through the viewfinder on the camera and began shouting directions at them. "Move closer together! Everyone shift half a foot to the left! That's too far — move back two inches to your right!"

"Take the damn picture!" Ryan commanded under his breath, in a voice too soft for the man to hear.

"You know, I've got some fifty-speed film in my car. I could just run up and grab it —"

"That's okay, really, if you could just take the picture," Marissa said.

"Please!" Summer added, as more of a command than a request.

"Fine." The man sighed, clearly disappointed on both a personal and an artistic level. He raised the camera to his eye again. "Okay, blond girl — angle your left foot forward. And you — Curly-top —"

"Is he talking to me?" Seth wondered.

"Yes, you. Pay attention! Now, put your arm around the girls and lean in slightly."

"Follow his directions and he might toss you a fish," Summer muttered.

And with that, the picture that the man finally took captured them all laughing, arms around one another, friendship preserved forever on the wrong speed film.

22

"Just think, this is the last bus ride we ever have to take," Summer said dreamily as the bus sped up the highway toward the finish line.

The best part of the scavenger hunt — other than helping the sick kids, of course — was that the adventure park that was a sponsor of the hunt was letting everyone who made it to the finish line in for free.

"Ha!" Seth said triumphantly. "I did it!"

"You did what?" Ryan asked.

"I broke the curse. I have traveled by bus with no bad consequences."

"We fought like a pack of wild dogs this weekend," Summer said, incredulous.

"Ah, yes, but we also kissed," Seth said.

"Shh!" Summer hissed, darting her eyes at Marissa and Ryan.

"Oh, like they don't know," Seth said. "Next you'll try to tell me you have no idea that Marissa and Ryan almost hooked up on that sub."

"You told him?!" Marissa said, giving Ryan the evil eye.

"Thanks, man," Ryan said to Seth.

"The *point*," Seth reiterated, "is that our fighting and our kissing cancel each other out, resulting in no more bad bus mojo for the Cohen-ator."

"There are so many things wrong with what you just said, I don't know where to start," Summer told him.

"Well, let's start with this: If I hurt your feelings or made you mad this weekend, it was accidental and I'm really sorry," Seth said. "That goes for all of you."

"I'm sorry that I yelled at you," Summer said, her whole body relaxing.

"I'm sorry, too," Marissa said, looking at each of her friends in turn.

"Me too," Ryan said. He was looking at his lap, but he rested his hand very gently on top of Marissa's. But —

"Want a hankie, you big girl?" Seth said to him.

Ryan blinked, taken aback, and Seth laughed.

"Come on, you guys, nothing *that* terrible happened this weekend. Sure, Summer revealed that she's still so crazy in love with me that she'll fly off the handle if another girl so much as *looks* at me —" Summer drew in an angry breath to retort, but Seth steamrolled right over her. "But it's not like Marissa OD'd, or Ryan set anyone's house on fire."

His friends stared at Seth, mouths agape, and

Seth broke up, laughing even harder. "I'm *joking*," he said.

Still none of the others laughed, so Seth pulled himself together. "Okay," he conceded, "let's remember the old adage — what happens on the scavenger hunt —"

". . . *Stays* on the scavenger hunt!" Marissa, Summer, and Ryan shouted. And all the ill feelings of the past three days were forgotten for good.

When the bus pulled into the parking lot, the four kids got a rush of adrenaline.

"We can still win this!" Marissa shouted, and they dashed for the entrance.

But when they got there, there was no sign of anyone from the charity waiting for them.

"What does this mean?" Summer asked. "What are we supposed to do?"

The kids looked around, and Marissa spotted something. "Look," she said to the others, reading off the small handbill posted on a bulletin board near the entrance. "'Scavenger hunters have nerves of steel.' Is that another clue?"

Just then, a white Taurus with Hertz plates screeched up to the entrance, and who should pile out but the Del Vista team!

"You!" Summer said, glaring at Autumn as though she might bite her.

Autumn ignored Summer, glancing around for a sign where to proceed next. She spotted the handbill and zipped over to read it.

Meanwhile, Felice sidled up to Seth. "Hi," she said.

"Hi," Seth answered, and both of them were met with betrayed glares from their teammates.

Seth looked at Summer, who was shooting daggers at him, then turned to Felice. "I'm sorry, but I think we need to break up," he told her.

"I understand," she answered in a sad soft voice.

"You guys, I got it!" Autumn shouted, and she and her team raced into the park, Felice casting one last longing backward glance at Seth.

Ryan shook his head to clear it, the meaning of the last clue instantly clear.

"It's the 'Superman the Escape' ride!" he shouted.

The Harbor kids went tearing into the park, desperate to beat Del Vista now, when it really counted.

They sprinted through the park, dodging little kids and old people, until they spotted the Superman ride ahead of them. There was a table set up in front of it, with dozens of balloons demarcating the official finish line.

As they skidded around the corner to reach it, the Del Vista team arrived, too. Both teams were about seventy-five feet away from the same smiley lady who had started the hunt, and with a bull-like roar, both teams started running as flat-out fast as they could to reach the finish first.

Mickey, who was so used to running wind-sprints

in football practice that he was barely breaking a sweat, decided to get creative. He reached out a meaty paw to push Ryan into the side of a building, but he overestimated his velocity.

Ryan easily dodged the shove, braking hard and using Mickey's momentum to grab his arm and let centrifugal force swing him around. As Mickey spun, a human wrecking ball, he took out Marissa, Summer, Autumn, and Chaz.

Only Seth and Felice were left standing. As they both ran toward the finish, Felice shot Seth a pleading, puppy-dog look: Pwease let me win.

Seth considered it for a second, then summoned every last reserve of strength inside him to put on a final burst of speed. He arrived at the finish mere seconds before Del Vista, and leaped into the air with joy, hollering and cheering as his teammates pulled themselves back to their feet and ran up to meet him.

"We won!" Seth shouted. "We won!"

"Actually?" the smiley woman said. "You're thirty-eighth."

"Out of how many teams?" Seth asked, suddenly sober.

The woman made an apologetic face. "Forty-two."

"Huh." The kids looked at one another for a long minute, digesting the news. Then —

"Ma'am? What place did Del Vista come in?"

"Thirty-ninth," the woman answered.

Summer stared at her, then started jumping up

and down again. "We won!" she shouted. "In your face, Autumn!"

Ryan and Marissa walked over to the judges' table. "So who actually won?" Ryan asked.

The judge checked her list. "A team Gummi Worms from Calabasas Prep."

"Cool," Ryan said, thinking of the annoying little talky kid and his friends. Little kids like that really cared about winning. For Ryan it was enough to have spent the time with his friends. Beating Del Vista didn't hurt, either.

"Congratulations on finishing, and thank you for the support you've given the A Dream to Share Foundation," the judge said. "Now go ride Superman the Escape and have fun."

Fun? Ryan stared up at the forty foot free-fall ride and felt his stomach drop away. His friends came up around him, and Seth slung an arm around his shoulders.

"Welcome to the scavenger hunt, bitch," he said.

And Seth, Summer, and Marissa coaxed Ryan to the back of the line, having hunted for clues and found their friendship all over again.

THE OC

'Twas the Night Before Chrismukkah

And all through the Newport mansions, not a creature was stirring except for Seth, Ryan, Marissa, and Summer. They're trying to spread some holiday cheer — without the use of credit cards or cash — but the holiday spirit is in short supply. It's going to take the miracle of Chrismukkah, and a few surprises, before these elves figure out how to save the holidays.

In bookstores December 2005